Dare, the Long Ride

Another Vantage Press title by the author:

Newtown

Dare, the Long Ride

Don Hopkins

VANTAGE PRESS
New York

This is a work of fiction. Any similarity between the names and characters in this book and any real persons, living or dead, is purely coincidental.

Cover design by Polly McQuillen

FIRST EDITION

Published by Vantage Press, Inc.
419 Park Ave. South, New York, NY 10016

Manufactured in the United States of America
ISBN: 978-0-533-16222-2

Library of Congress Catalog Card No: 2009902726

0 9 8 7 6 5 4 3 2 1

To my two daughters, Donna and Donica. Thank you for being you, says it all.

Acknowledgment

Thank you to my granddaughter, Dainna Tyler, for all her help in making this book possible and to my brother, Darrel, for all his help.

Dare, the Long Ride

1

Red brought his tin plate of beans from the chuck wagon and sat down beside me and started spooning them in. I was already halfway through my plateful when the cook called over from the chuck wagon and said, "Hey boys, the beefsteaks are ready to eat. You had better come and get them now before they turn into shoe leather."

Red turned his week-old-unshaven face toward the cook, and said, "Cookie, why don't you take those goddamn beefsteaks and stuff them up your you know where."

Cookie responded with a big happy laugh, and said, "You would think you boys don't like beef that had just walked over a hundred miles. Hell's bells, these steaks are all meat and bones without an ounce of fat left on them."

Red returned his attention back to his plate of beans and said, to no one in particular, "If you ask mc, that goddamn cook has a sick sense of humor. We've been following those goddamn steers all the way from Texas and all I can recall about the whole spring trip is steer shit, piss, and then, on top of all that, you have to put up with them constantly stinking up the air."

"Hell," Red continued, "I've had to get up in the middle of the night just so I could ride circles around those stupid critters so that I could sing to the dumb sons-of-bitches."

I laughed and said, "Don't forget, Red, the time they stampeded in the middle of the night."

"Don't you worry about me forgetting about that. I was on night duty when they decided to run for no goddamn reason that anyone can figure out and then they had the audacity to try their damnest to run me down. The only reason I'm alive to talk about it is because I'm such a damn good horseman. I'll never eat beef again even if it means I have to eat beans and biscuits for the rest of my life."

"Hell, Red," I said "you haven't even mentioned the two spring snowstorms we had to drive the cattle through."

"Don't you worry about me forgetting about that. I goddamn near froze my ass off in those storms just so we could be the first herd to market."

Red had me laughing by the time he got over his rampage and I was barely able to say, "Maybe you should go over there and shoot the cook just for the hell of it."

By this time Red was also laughing but was able to say, "I might just do that when I'm finished with these delicious beans. I know it would make me feel better."

Red and I had been partnered up now for five years. Red was about thirty-three and I was seventeen when I first met him. Since the day I met Red, he has been like a father to me.

2

I don't know my biological parents and was raised in a orphanage in New York City until I was sixteen. A lot of people will tell you how bad it is to be raised in an orphanage and I'm sure some orphanages are worse than others, but in my case, I had no memory of what a real home was like so for me it wasn't all that bad. Sure, there were a lot of rules and I must have broken each one of them at one time or another and some of them more than once. The punishment, if you were caught, was swift and harsh but I'm sure it had to be that way with so many scheming young boys around always trying to raise hell.

When I was very young, I would hear grown-ups talk about the West. Being young, in my mind the West was a place of freedom and open country and it drew me in like a fly to honey and gave me a goal in life. That goal was that one day, I knew that I was going to head west.

It also helped in my schoolwork because I wanted to learn more about the West and the only way I could do that was to learn how to read. As soon as I had accomplished that, I would read and reread everything that I could lay my hands on about the West. I was so fixed on the subject, I knew for a fact that I had to head west.

At the age of sixteen, I was allowed to leave the orphanage, and with the orphanage's help, I was able to land a job driving a horse trailer for a city delivery service. The pay wasn't much but the job worked out well for me and for the company that hired me.

The company warehouse had a small room in the

back and I was allowed to stay there free of charge. I had a free place to live and the company received a free night watchman.

The cost of food was minimal because of the type of deliveries I made. Most were edible items such as potatoes, eggs, fresh vegetables and such and a lot of that seemed to find their way into my pockets by the end of the day.

I saved every dime that I could. In just a little over a year, I had saved enough to buy an old broken-down horse, a well used old rusty rifle, a saddle that had seen better days, and enough food to last a few days. With all that wealth, I quit my job and headed west to fulfill my big dream. I had no set destination in mind when I rode out of New York, but I did know what direction west was and that's the direction I headed.

I was a wise-ass kid of seventeen, but a man in my mind, fresh from the streets of New York, who thought he could take care himself.

The way I had it figured, as soon as I got out of the New York area, I would be able to hunt for my food. I learned mighty fast that hunting so close to civilization was not all that easy. In fact, when my limited supplies ran low, most of my food came from free handouts and what I was able to steal out of farmers' gardens at night.

All in all, I was happy. I was heading west and the way I had it figured, things could only get better the further west I went and I was doing it on my own without help from anyone other than the free handouts.

This attitude lasted until I was about a hundred or so miles out of New York, on a lonely road between towns. It was there that I met up with four men who showed me that I was nothing but a dumb-ass kid.

Those old boys did a real number on me. They took

everything I owned that was worth taking, which included my limited supplies, my horse, what little change there was in my pocket, and my rifle. They even took my hat and boots. They worked me over pretty good and left me half-dead alongside the trail. I still hoped that the day will come when I will cross paths with one or more of those boys.

3

Red was the one that found me and nursed me back to health. If it hadn't been for him, I believe I would have just curled up and died where I lay. Since that day five years ago, Red and I have been riding together.

I polished off that last of my beans and took my tin plate and cup over to the chuck wagon. Before dropping my plate into the large pan of water placed on the tailgate of the chuck wagon for that purpose, I used my spoon to scrape my plate free of any scraps into a small hole that had been dug next to one of the wheels along side the chuck wagon. The hole would be covered with dirt after all the hands had eaten and a new hole dug for the next meal. I often wondered how many spoons were buried across the country during trail drives. I knew that if I dropped my spoon in that slop, I sure as hell wouldn't dig for it. The holes were only dug when we were staying in one place longer than normal during the drive. During the drive, we would take our noon breaks in small groups so that we could keep the herd moving. The only exception to that was when we bedded down the steers for the night. Then we would have supper and breakfast in the same location. Under those conditions, we would just scrape our plates clean in the prairie and let the small animals take care of the clean-up duties.

Now that we were held up for a few days waiting for the herd to be sold and shipped we used the slop hole. Because the weather was starting to get hot during the day, we sure as hell didn't need scraps of food laying around camp stinking up the place. About a day of that and the place would soon be unbearable.

After cleaning my plate, I refilled my cup with coffee and returned to my saddle, where I had been sitting. Soon after that, Red got up and took his plate to the chuck wagon. While I was sitting there sipping coffee, I heard Red start cussing out the cook. The way the cook was laughing, I figured he was trying to dish up a big steak for Red.

The cook was still laughing when Red returned with his cup and sat down in the same spot next to me. After a few minutes of silence, Red asked, "Where the hell did Indian get off to? I haven't seen him since we started to put the cattle in the stock pens for shipment back east. Now that I think on it, he vanished early this morning even before we started moving those stupid animals down to the shipping pens." After a moment he added, "Just like him to take off when there's work to be done."

"Hell, Red ," I said, "the trail boss hired him to scout the trail ahead of the herd to locate water and good locations to bed the herd down at night. Besides that if it hadn't been for him bringing in fresh meat now and then, those bean meals would have gotten mighty old. God forbid we might shoot one of those steers for meat while we were on the drive. The only reason the boss had that steer butchered today was due to the fact it was so skinny and scrawny-looking. He was afraid that if any of the buyers were to have a look at him it would have driven the price down on the whole herd."

Red scratched his gray old beard and nodded his head in agreement and said, "That sure was one scrawny-looking steer, wasn't it? If it had been left up to me, I would have been too damn embarrassed to have him butchered for meat. I think I would have run that poor excuse for a steer out into the prairie and let the wolves have at him."

I could tell Red was still smarting about riding drag during the drive. We all took our turns at riding drag and I'm sure we all felt that we had held down that job more than our fair share. It was the dirtiest job on the cattle drive and no one cared for it. No matter how hard you tried to keep your hanky over your nose and mouth and the top button on your shirt done up, the dust would find its way in. By the time you finished your tour on drag, your eyes would be burning and every time you blowed your nose, for the next couple of days, all you would get was dust.

I pulled out my bag of tobacco and rolled a smoke and then offered the makings over to Red who accepted and made one for himself. We sat there for a time in silence, enjoying our smokes, before Red said, "Where did that Indian take off for? Hell, the drive is over so there's no need for him to be out scouting. I sure hope he gets back before you and I pull out."

"I heard him say something about getting some fresh meat," I answered.

Red shook his head and looked into the prairie before he said, "I sure don't see what he will find out there in that dried-out prairie land. Probably only find those floppy-eared, long-legged jackrabbits that we seemed to be herding along with the cattle the last few weeks. The little sons-of-bitches jumped out and spooked my horse a couple of times and I damn near got thrown. Once again it was only due to my great skills as a horseman that I was able to stay in the saddle."

I had to laugh as I said, "Red, you sure like to toot your own horn sometimes."

"Shit, Dell, if I don't who the hell would do it for me?"

I glanced out west of the camp and could see Indian riding in. I nodded my head in that direction and said to Red, "If jackrabbits are the only thing out there, as you claim, it sure looks like Indian found one big enough to hang over his saddle and it's also the first time I've seen a jackrabbit with antlers. Hell, they don't even grow jackrabbits that big down in Texas."

4

Neither Red nor I had known Indian when we had hired on at the start of the cattle drive. For Red and me, this was our second cattle drive so you would have thought that we should have known better than to sign on again. But, when you are flat-ass broke, you tend to forget that after the first drive you had sworn that you would never sign on for another dirt-eating cattle drive again.

Indian had signed on for the second drive as the scout and also to supply fresh meat for the crew.

You would think with all the cattle we were driving to the railhead, fresh meat would be the least of our worries. However, God forbid that a steer be lost due to butchering. That was money out of the trail boss's pocket, because he got a share of the profit at the end of the drive for each steer that made it to market. The scout was paid for by the herd's owners. As far as the trail boss was concerned, the crew could eat beans the whole goddamn trip if the scout couldn't find fresh meat. We had been lucky on this drive because Indian always seemed to be able to locate fresh meat when it was needed.

From what little we had been able to learn from Indian, he preferred to be just called Indian and he had been raised by two well-educated elderly white folks who not only taught him to read and write but also worked him very hard, so as they put it, "He could earn his keep." At the age of thirteen he had borrowed one of the white folks' horses, without their knowledge, and struck out on his own. After a few years of looking the country over and at the same time trying to find his roots, he signed up with the army as a scout for several years. It was just after he completed his last contract with the army that he signed on for the cattle drive.

At the start of the drive, he stayed pretty much to himself, but I couldn't fault him for that because Red and I stayed pretty much to ourselves also. After time, Indian started to bring his coffee over in the evening and would sit with us as we drank our last cup of the day. In time, he started to roll out his bedroll in our general area. From that time on, while we were on the drive, the three of us kind of stuck together.

When Indian rode up to the chuck wagon with the fresh kill, he slid the deer off the front of his saddle onto the ground. As he climbed down from his horse, Cookie said, "You could have skinned the deer out before you brought it in."

Indian tied his horse to the check wagon wheel and removed his saddle and, without looking at cook, said, "That's work for women and cooks, not for warriors."

I could hear Red snickering beside me. I think he was happy to hear someone giving the cook a hard time after the cook had tried to pawn off one of those lean beef steaks on him.

The cook glared at Indian but didn't say anything. I believe most of the cowhands including the cook were a little bit scared of Indian.

Indian carried his saddle over to where Red and I were sitting and dropped it on the ground then returned to the chuck wagon and poured himself a cup of coffee and walked back and sat down beside us. After a few sips of coffee he said, "I see you got those stupid critters to the loading pens." Around Red and me, Indian spoke perfect

English and I'll be the first to admit he spoke it better than Red or me.

"Stupid is right," Red said with conviction. I reckon he was still thinking about all the time he had spent on drag during the long drive.

I added to the conversation by telling Indian, "The boss is in town arranging for the sale of the cattle with the buyers and getting an advance to pay us off."

Indian took a few sips of his coffee and asked, "Are you boys planning to head for town when you get paid off?"

Red spoke up and said, "I can't speak for Dell, but I sure as hell am not going back to that goddamn town after the little trouble we had there last year."

"What do you mean by a little trouble?" I asked. "I seem to recall a whole lot of trouble."

"Maybe so," Red said with a smile on his face and then added, "but it sure was fun the first couple of days."

"If you don't mind my asking, what did happen?" Indian asked.

Red didn't say anything so it was left up to me to fill Indian in on what had taken place the last time we were in town. I drank the last of my coffee and dumped the coffee grinds and proceeded to tell Indian what had transpired a year ago this month.

"When Red and I got paid off at the end of last year's drive we decided to go into town for a few drinks. Those few drinks turned into a big party that lasted for the next two days. The first two days were nothing but a good time. Hell, we had money; there was a lot of drinking, plenty of gambling, and more than a few ladies always available. On the morning of the third day, three of the local boys decided that we were monopolizing the saloon ladies a little too much and they requested that we move on out of town and down the trail."

Before continuing with my story, I looked over at Red for a moment then added, "I don't recall for sure who threw the first punch, but for the next ten minutes all hell broke loose in the saloon. By the time the city marshal arrived, Red and I were still standing. Because the three boys that were lying on the floor were local boys and Red and I were from the cattle drive, we were the only ones arrested and thrown in jail.

"After a week in the can, we had our day in court. We were sentenced to the time served and fined for disorderly conduct plus cost of repairs to the saloon and given three hours to get out of town. The marshal also strongly suggested that we never return to his town. We pooled what little money we had left to pay off our feed bill at the livery stable and high-tailed it out of there.

"We understand that they still have the same marshal in town so we have decided to ride to a small town about seventy miles west of here called Forks. From what we hear, the town is big enough to have a restaurant and a saloon where we can get some good food and have a few drinks. After that, we plan to buy supplies and head on west to do a little gold prospecting. Besides, we've never seen that part of the country before."

Indian nodded his head and said, "Sounds like a good plan."

Red and I had talked it over earlier and wondered if Indian wanted to ride along with us but decided to just tell him what our plans were and if he should care to ride along it would be up to him. We figured that we could sure use him because the territory we were planning to head into was Indian land and Indian had a lot of experience in that line of work while scouting for the army.

5

We were still sitting there when the trail boss returned from town and we had no more time to discuss our plans with Indian.

A small table and stool were taken from the chuck wagon and set up in the shady side of the wagon. The trail boss sat down and laid out a stack of gold coins and several stacks of silver coins. As soon as he was set up, he opened his tally book and started to call our names. As each rider's name was called out, he would step up to the table and sign his name or place his mark in the tally book and the boss would pay him off, shake the rider's hand and thank him.

Red was the first of us three to be called up the table to sign his name and receive his pay. He was proud when he picked up the pen and printed RED in bold letters, and received his pay. Red had never had any schooling so he couldn't read or write when I met him. At his request, I had shown him how to print RED so, as he put it, he wouldn't be embarrassed when he had to put his mark to paper. I tried to teach him more but he said he wasn't interested. All he wanted to know was enough so that he wouldn't have to put down an "X" for his name.

Indian was called up next and wrote down INDIAN and I have to say his penmanship was much better then mine.

I was next in line and could have written out my full name but I figured no one would know who it was if they should look at the tally book later so I just signed DELL.

Less than an hour later, Red, Indian and I were saddling up our horses. Most of the hands had left for town and we had said our good-byes as they rode out. Some of the crew, that had families waiting for them back down south, would return in a couple of hours and would follow the boss and the chuck wagon back down the trail to home. A good percentage of the ones that remained in town after the boss had headed south would either end up broke, in jail, or run out of town when their money ran out. The trail herd riders were always welcome in the cattle town as long as they stayed on their side of town, where there were several saloons, and they had money in their pockets.

The trail boss came by as we were just finishing saddling our horses and about ready to ride out. He stopped and said, "You three did a fine job on the drive and if you make it down south early next spring, look me up. I should have another herd put together by then and I would be happy to sign you boys on for another drive."

"I'll be gone to hell, if I will ever sign on for another goddamn cattle drive," Red said with meaning, and then added, "That is meant with no disrespect to you, boss."

The trail boss laughed at Red's remarks and said, "None taken, Red." I think he had heard the same words many times before. In fact, I believe I had heard Red say the very same thing last year as we finished up that drive. It sure is surprising how you can forget what you had promised yourself, just a few months back, when you were broke and hungry.

Before the boss walked away, I asked, "Boss, do you have a spare horse that we could buy? We are in need of a good pack animal and don't care to go into town for one."

"Sure, pick a horse from our spare mounts and then we can dicker over the price. But if you boys want to save a little money, you can have that mule that is ground-staked over yonder." The boss pointed out a mule but he really didn't have to because we all knew which mule he was referring to, Old Pain-in-the-Ass, as the riders started to call him and for good reasons. About fifty percent of the time when you went to fetch him in the morning he would be gone. It didn't seem to matter how secure you thought you had him at night, there was a mighty good chance he would be gone in the morning. Sometimes he would work at the knot until he had himself untied and if that didn't work he could always chew his way through the rope. The damn mule would have been cut loose long ago if it wasn't for the fact that once he was loaded he would follow along like a dog and go all day without a break. For some unknown reason, he just seemed to like to roam about at night. He never wandered far from camp but it was still a pain in the ass to have to go looking for him every morning.

When we hesitated, the boss said, "I was planning on chaining him to the back of the chuck wagon and dragging him all the way back down to Texas but if you boys would take him off my hands it would be doing me a big favor."

When the boss put it that way we accepted his offer and as we rode out we stopped long enough to put a rope on Old Pain-in-the-Ass and the three of us, along with Old Pain-in-the Ass, set off.

Indian never did say he would ride along with us but then he had never said that he wouldn't. However, I was happy to see him take the lead as our small group headed west.

6

The first day out we took our time as the horses weren't all that fresh due to the trail drive. We decided to move slow and make frequent stops whenever we came across good grazing. We also made camp early so the horses could rest and eat their fill.

The next morning we spent an hour looking for Old Pain-in the-Ass. We finally found him about ten feet from where we had started looking. When we got up and saw that he was missing, Indian and I had set out looking for him. Indian was good at reading signs and we were able to follow him straight out of camp where he made a big circle around the perimeter of the camp and by the time we caught up with him he was back with the rest of the horses, happily eating grass. He certainly had the right name, "Pain-in-the-Ass."

We continued at a slow pace on the second day also, and figured we would reach Forks around midday of the third day.

It was about noon of our second day out, that dark clouds started to build to the west of us. I watched the clouds build for the rest of the day, but they didn't seem to be moving our way a whole lot. However, being the prudent man that I am, I said, "We had better sleep under our rain gear tonight."

Red said, "I've been watching the clouds off and on all day and they're not moving our way. I think it will pass west of us tonight." Then he made a big show of smelling the air and added, "I can smell rain a good day ahead of time and I don't smell anything." He then looked over at Indian and asked, "What you do think, Indian, is it going to rain on us tonight?"

Indian looked at the sky west of us and took a deep breath and then said, "The rain won't reach us until sometime late tomorrow."

Red looked over at me and said, "There, are you satisfied Dell? Indian said it's not going to rain tonight, and it's a well-known fact that Indians can tell the weather better than anyone."

"That may be so," I answered Red, "but I'm setting up my wet weather gear before I crawl into my bedroll tonight."

"Go ahead and do all the work of setting up, but I'll be sound asleep long before you get it set up."

It was around midnight when the rain started, and it came in a hard downpour for the rest of the night. All three of us were crowded under my small shelter which now allowed only room to sit up. I was sitting in the middle between Red and Indian and I was keeping relatively dry. However, with each gust of wind, I knew Red and Indian were getting wetter by the minute.

After several minutes of watching the downpour, I asked Red, "Red is that the rain that you said would pass west of us during the night that's coming down hard on your side?"

"Don't be a smart-ass, Dell, you know goddamn well how hard it's coming down."

Several more minutes passed before I felt it was time to stick it to them again and I said, "I seem to recall that you boys said it wasn't going to rain tonight."

"It was Indian who said it wouldn't rain until late tomorrow and it's a goddamn well-known fact that Indians are suppose to be able to forecast the weather," Red said as he tried to shift all the blame onto Indian.

After a moment, Indian answered Red's accusations by saying, in what he considered to be a limited knowledge of the English language, "I watch the old Red-headed one, who is a great frontiersman and a famous legend among my Red brothers. He smelled the air and then spoke that there would not be any rain this night. I knew he was wrong but I agreed with him so that I could show great respect for the old one, which is the Indian custom." After a short pause Indian added, this time in his own voice, "Besides, what the hell would make you think I know anything more about the weather than you two do."

Again there was a long pause before Red spoke up and said, "There is one bit of truth in all that bullshit from Indian."

"What's that?" I asked.

"I am a famous legend among the Indians and I'm sure they are singing their praises of me over their campfires."

All I could get out was, "Shit," and started laughing and was soon joined by my two companions. If any riders were to pass by our camp and seen three wet grown men huddled under a one-man lean-to, laughing ourselves silly, they sure as hell would have kept on riding, thinking that we were completely out of our minds and probably dangerous.

It was just starting to get light when the rain turned to a light drizzle and the wind let up to the point where we were able to roll ourselves smokes without them getting soaking wet. The smoke seemed to take the edge off things and we didn't feel quite so miserable.

By the time it was light enough to move around camp

we decided to break camp. A fire and a cup coffee would have tasted mighty good but with everything wet, including us, the effort didn't seem worth it. We figured we would probably hit the town of Forks around noon and then we could have coffee and something to eat.

The only problem with our plan was the fact that Old Pain-in-the-Ass was gone. Due to all the rain during the night his trail was impossible to find. After a quick look around and the fact that we were all so miserable from being wet Red said, "I say to hell with the son-of-a-bitch. If we are going to have to chase down that piece of crow bait every morning, I'm for leaving him for the wolves. We can pick up a pack horse when we buy our supplies in town."

I have to admit it sure wasn't a problem to either Indian or me as we both nodded our heads in agreement.

When we were about ready to move out, I glanced over my shoulder and there was Old Pain-in-the-Ass only a few paces from us. When I pointed that fact out to my two companions, Red said, "I should just shoot the stupid animal and we would be done with it."

I thought it over for moment then said, "If he follows us all the way to town, we can use him for trade and get a pack horse a little bit cheaper."

"Goddamn it, Dell, all you ever think about is how to save a buck. Besides that you will be throwing a screw into anyone who takes him for trade."

At this point Indian put in his two cents worth, "I'm for trading him. It would make me happy to think that he is hooked to the front end of a plow for the rest of his life. I'm sick of hunting him down every other morning."

Red, after a moment in deep thought, said, "Indian's point is well-taken. I withdraw my plan to shoot him."

7

We found that we were closer to the town of Forks than we had previously thought. The sun, which was still on our backs, made the time about ten A.M., well ahead of our estimated noon arrival time.

As soon as we reached the edge of town, you could see how the town had gotten its name. Just before you entered the town, the road that we were on forked off in two directions. One of the roads headed north and the other continued west. The town itself was built on the west road after you passed the fork in the road. My guess is that the town was built on the west road because the town got most of its business from folks passing through heading west. The town itself wasn't much and I'm sure that if the travelers passing by found a better route, the town would dry up and blow away. The town did have a livery stable, saloon, general store, and we were later to learn from the stable man, a small place to eat.

Our first stop in town was at the small livery stable where we put up our horses and requested a stall that had a gate with a drop bar so we could pen Old Pain-in-the-Ass in and lock the gate. For two bits per head the horses would be given grain along with a good supply of hay. Reluctantly we added two bits more for Old Pain-in-the-Ass.

Normally after being on the trail for a few days our first stop would have been the saloon. However, seeing how we had missed food and coffee this morning, due to the rain that wasn't supposed to have fallen on us, we asked the stable man about food and then followed his direction to a small greasy spoon down the street, a couple doors past the saloon.

From the outside, the only indication that this was indeed a place to eat was a paper sign in the front window that stated, in big letters, MEALS. The menu listed what was available and the prices. For breakfast you had a choice of steak and eggs or bacon and eggs. From twelve o'clock on, your choice were steak or venison, depending on what was available. All meals came with coffee, fried potatoes and bread.

The moment we sat down an old-timer placed three cups on the table and a hot pot of coffee and then took our orders. We each ordered the same thing: a double order of eggs with bacon and fried potatoes. I guess we still hadn't gotten over our dislike of beef. Then we each poured a cup of coffee which was hot and black. In a very short time we poured our second round of coffees, built ourselves smokes, leaned back in our chairs, and sipped our coffee while enjoying our smokes until our food arrived.

After finishing our food and a second pot of coffee, we headed over to the saloon for a drink, and if we were lucky, any news about what was happening around the area. As it happened, we didn't hear any news and the whiskey, on a scale of one to ten, was about five.

There were five men in the saloon, including the bartender, and none of them looked friendly. Three were sitting at a table in the corner of the room playing cards and one man standing at the bar talking to the bartender.

While Red and Indian walked over to a table, I walked to the bar and bought a bottle and picked up three glasses then walked over to the table that Red and Indian had picked out.

We poured a round and lifted our glasses to one another as Red said, “Here’s to us,” and we downed our first shot of what could only be referred to as rotgut stomach-burning whiskey. After a moment of silence while we caught our breath and smacked our lips, we poured a second round. As we sipped on our second glass of whiskey, we all rolled smokes and sat back and relaxed. Hell, we had been on the trail for three days and now we had full stomachs, a bottle of whiskey and were among friends. I ask you, what more could one ask for other than being left alone by strangers?

Like most good things, this didn’t last for long. The man standing at the bar said, “Shit,” which was meant to be loud enough for us to hear. He then turned our way and said, “We don’t serve Indians in here.”

We sat there as if we hadn’t heard him and continued to sip our whiskey and talk.

After a full minute, when we hadn’t responded to his statement, he probably took it that we were afraid of a confrontation with him. With his confidence rising by the minute, due to our lack of response and the whiskey that he had put away, he swaggered over to our table and looked down at Indian and repeated, “I said, we don’t serve your kind in this saloon.”

I looked up at him and asked, “Which one of us are you referring to?”

Glancing at me he said, “I’m talking to the Indian, you goddamn fool.”

“The reason I asked is because the three of us are blood brothers. We should get everything straightened out before the shooting starts.”

“I agree with Dell about getting all the little details straight,” Red said. “I sure don’t want any misunderstanding after the shooting is over.”

The stranger stood there shaking his head and looking at us like we weren't right in our minds. To get control of the conversation he said, "We have a saying around here that the only good Indian is a dead Indian."

In a very casual voice, Indian said, "That is very strange. My people have a very similar saying that goes something like, the only good white man is a dead white man."

The stranger had never been talked to like that by an Indian and was at the point of drawing his pistol when I said, to no one in particular, "If all three of us shoot him, who gets the rights to claim the kill?"

You could tell by the stranger's posture that he felt that he was starting to lose control of what was going on around him. Before he could recover from that remark, Red added a little more to the conversation. "If I shot him twice, I think I should get to claim the kill. How does that sound to you two?"

Indian said, "That would be okay with me. Keeping count of one's kills is a white man thing. I guess you and Dell will have to figure it out after he is dead."

The stranger was breaking out in a sweat and was fast coming down from his whiskey high. Looking first at Red and then over at me he said "I have no quarrel with you two boys; I just want you to know we don't serve Indians in here."

Red asked him, "Are you the owner of this fine establishment? When the man shook his head no, Red said, "Then why don't you just piss off?"

The stranger stood there with his hand within an inch or two from his pistol grip, but he was no longer so sure of himself. So I decided to help him make up his mind, and I said, "Mister, the moment your hand touches that pistol you're going to have three mighty big holes in you. I'm not much of a betting man but right now I would be willing to bet that your pistol never clears leather."

The stranger stood there with the sweat starting to run down his face and a second later his hand moved away from his pistol grip. He swallowed hard and then said, in a very dry voice, "Hell, boys, I have no quarrel with any of you. I was just passing on what I thought was general policy." As he was talking he was walking backward and when he was about six feet from our table he turned and headed for the door. By the time he hit the swinging doors of the saloon he was almost running. He must have had his horse tied out front of the saloon because a moment later we could hear a rider heading down the street at a hard run.

We poured another round of drinks from our bottle and all was quiet. The three at the card table were looking our way but soon went back to their cards. The bartender was doing "make work" polishing the glasses and pretending that he hadn't heard anything.

A few minutes of silence passed before Red picked up the tobacco and started to roll a smoke, and said, "Have you noticed how much more a man smokes while he is drinking? I wonder why that is."

The incident with the stranger, no longer being a concern, was forgotten.

8

After we had polished off half the whiskey, we picked the bottle up and headed over to the general store for the supplies we were going to need.

We found the shelves well-stocked with items that were ideal to meet our need for travel and prospecting. The prices were a little on the high side but one had to expect that this far from the main supply centers.

The main items on our list were items that would not turn bad while we were traveling. They included a side of cured bacon, dried beans, corn, peas, flour, coffee and a good supply of beef jerky. To this we added the other essentials that were required for cooking such as salt and baking powder so that we could whip up a pan of biscuits when needed. For cooking utensils we added a large steel frying pan and a large steel stew pot. The pot would come in handy for making stew which was easy to make. Hell, all you had to do was add water and good piece of meat, then throw in a handful of whatever dried food you had around the camp. Set the pot next to the fire and walk away and when you came back later you would have your meal ready and waiting for you. Then if you were going to stay in the same spot for a few days, you could always fill the pot a little fuller with odds and ends and you only had to add a few more dried items after you had eaten and then you could continue to eat from the pot for a couple of more days.

We already had a coffee pot so that wasn't on the list. The last few items on our list were things that we would need if we were going to look for gold. They included three gold-panning pans, a pick and two shovels. The last thing we purchased was ammunition. We all carried the same caliber weapons so we only needed one type of ammunition. We decided that with the rounds we already had, we would need four more boxes, but in the end, to be on the safe side, we added two more, bringing it to a total of six boxes.

We bagged all our supplies and headed back to the livery stable to store the items with our saddles until we were ready to ride out and, if possible, spend the night in the hayloft, seeing how there was no hotel in town. It was also time to see if we could unload Old Pain-in-the-Ass for a good pack horse. The damn mule had been in the stable long enough for the stable man to see that he was friendly and easy to handle. He wouldn't have had time to figure out that Old Pain-in-the-Ass liked nothing better than to roam around, on his own, at night.

While we were making arrangements for spending the night in the stable, Red brought up the subject about trading Old Pain-in-the-Ass by asking the stableman, "You don't know where we could trade our mule for a good pack horse do you?"

The stableman looked at him like he might be losing his mind and asked, "Why the hell do you want to trade a good pack mule for a horse or is there something wrong with him?"

It was time for Red to get the ball rolling, and he said, "There's nothing wrong with the mule; it's the damn Indian who is with us who is the problem."

The stable man looked over at the Indian who was standing with his arms folded across his chest trying to look like one of those fierce looking wooden Indians you see in front of stores back east. I think the look Indian was going for was what he considered a wild Indian just off the reservation would look like, as he said, "I am a warrior and warriors do not ride with mules. Mules only good for eating."

Me, I had turned away to keep from laughing and spoiling the deal. Red was left to carry on the conversation with a straight face and he said, "You see the spot that we are in. I'm afraid one day out on the trail, the damn Indian might get hungry for mule meat, and you can see how that could leave us high and dry."

The stable man started to get that look where he was thinking, maybe I can make some money here, but wasn't quite ready to accept what he was hearing so he asked what he thought was the logical question. "Why don't you just get rid of the damn Indian?"

For a moment there I thought he had Red, but Red came through with flying colors as he said, without hesitation, "I would sure like to get shook of the goddamn Indian but we are heading into Indian Territory and he might come in handy if we have to deal with some wild Indians. God knows he isn't worth shit around camp."

At that point you could see that the stable man was sold on the idea. He stood there for a time scratching his beard as if he wasn't sure he wanted to make any kind of trade but finally said, "I suppose we might work something out." His hesitation had been for our benefit.

"I'll tell you what, boys. Out back of the stable, I have three horses in the corral. You can go take a look and if you find one that you like come on back and maybe we can make a deal."

In the end we did make a deal. The stable man believed that he had pulled a fast one on two dumb cowboys and an equally dumb Indian. Hell, we were happy; we ended up with a good pack horse at a very reasonable price and at the same time got rid of Old Pain-in-the-Ass.

After all our gear was stowed away and while the stable man was still there to watch over our supplies, we headed back to the restaurant where we had eaten our breakfast and had an early supper. Normally one would not have to worry about his gear, but this far out a man's horse and supplies could mean life or death. Your supplies ranged right up there with the value one places on his horse.

After our early supper, we found three stools in the livery stable, and set them outside the stable doors and sat down. We spent the evening telling lies, smoking and sipping from the bottle of whiskey we had taken from the saloon earlier. The stable man joined us for couple of drinks, before he set out for a small ranch he had outside of town. We said we would see him in the morning as we planned to have breakfast before we pulled out and said good night and he headed for home.

It was getting along about dusk and we were still out in front of the stable enjoying the coolness of the evening when the three men who had been playing cards in the saloon earlier in the day rode back into town. They gave us a good once-over as they rode by the stable. After dismounting in front of the saloon, they went inside. A short time later they came out and stood in front of the saloon talking something over and occasionally one would glance our way. They continued their conversation for about ten minutes outside the saloon and then one left the group and headed for the general store. He was only in the store for a very short time, before he walked back to the front of the saloon where his two friends stood. After a short conversation, the three entered the saloon.

Red said, "Those boys sure seemed to be very interested in us."

"That they did," I answered.

Red stripped his smoke out and then ground it into dirt with the heel of his boot. "You know," he said, "I think after it gets a little darker, I might slip over to the general store and have a talk with the clerk."

"You know, Red, that may not be a bad idea."

As soon as the sun went down and it started to get dark, Red walked into the dark stable and went out the back door and made his way, using the dark shadows, to the general store. Twenty minutes later he was back sitting with us and repeated what the store clerk told him. "He said the one that came into the store had bought a sack of tobacco but then seemed to have more interest in if we had been in and when he found out we had been, he seemed very interested in what we had bought. The clerk said he didn't tell him much but I wouldn't put much stock in that. The clerk seems to be one who likes to talk. He said the three rode into town about four days ago, and they seem to be mighty short on cash."

After we had killed the bottle, it was full dark so we climbed into the hayloft and made ourselves comfortable. Because of all the interest shown in us by the three strangers, we decided that we should take turns staying awake so that one of us would be awake to watch over our supplies. To determine who pulled what time slots, we drew straws. Indian got the first shift with Red second and I got the last watch. Indian and I were happy with the outcome; however, Red did a lot of cussing before he went to sleep. When your watch is in the middle of the night it means you have to get up from a sound sleep, do your watch and then try to get back to sleep after your two hours or so of guard duty was done, which at times can be hard to do. Of course, our laughing at Red's bad luck didn't help and we had to endure Red's hard words that were directed at us. On the first shift of guard duty one only had to stay up a while longer than normal and the one on the last shift of guard duty, which was mine, meant that I would only be getting up a little earlier than usual. Being an early riser, the idea of getting up a couple hours earlier than normal didn't bother me.

We didn't have any problems until it was my turn to hold down guard duty. I was sitting there thinking about getting up and stepping outside the stable so that I could have a smoke, when I heard the squeak of the stable doors being opened. As soon as one of the stable doors was open, I could see three men, with the moonlight in back of them, step through the door and enter the stable. I recognized them as the three who had been playing cards in the saloon last evening and had made the stop at general store. While they were still silhouetted by the open stable door, I levered a round into the chamber of my rifle and before they could make their way into the dark shadows of the stable I asked, "Are you boys looking for something." By the time I finished asking the question, you could hear Red and the Indian levering rounds in their weapons also.

The three froze in place. They couldn't see us and they knew that they were silhouetted in the open door. I'm sure the sound of rounds being levered into the rifles had a lot to do with their standing so still.

After a long pause, one of them in the doorway said, "We were looking for a place to bed down for the night." This didn't ring true because it would be starting to get light very soon.

"We are all full up boys," Red said, "looks like you're a might bit late."

"Well, then. We will be moving on and make camp

outside of town," responded one of the strangers from below, as they turned and headed for the door.

"Be sure to close the door on your way out, boys," Red added.

It wasn't long after the three strangers left, that Red and Indian were back sound asleep. It was as if nothing had happened. I sat there for another half hour and then climbed down from the hayloft and slipped out of the stable and had that smoke I had been thinking about when I had been disturbed.

When I slipped out of the stable door, you could just see the eastern sky starting to change from black to a washed-out gray.

9

I was sitting on one of the stools in front of the stable, having my second smoke when the sun was just starting to peek over the skyline and I was soaking up the first warm rays of the sun. The morning was chilly but it felt good because I knew that soon it would be another very hot day.

As I was sitting there enjoying the fresh air and the start of another day, the livery stable man rode up and dismounted in front of the stable. After waving a good morning, he swung the stable door open wide and took his horse inside, and after a few minutes he returned, sat down beside me and rolled his own smoke, and said, “You’re up and about early this morning.”

“Yep,” I answered, “I’ve always been an early riser.” I didn’t feel the need to tell him we ran three strangers out of his livery stable early this morning.

After another pause, I asked, “What time does the eating place open in the morning?”

“That kind of depends on how much the cook drank last night. Every so often, he will go on an all-night drunk, and if that was the case last night, he won’t open till late this afternoon and only then if he feels well enough to open at all.”

“What do you figure the odds are of my partners and me getting fed this morning?” I asked.

Scratching his beard in deep thought, he said, “Let me see, it was last Monday he went on his last toot and usually his toots run on about a weekly cycle, so I would say the odds of getting fed for the next couple of days would be pretty good."

About this time, I could hear movement inside the stable and then heard someone cursing and I figured Red was up and about with no coffee in sight.

Five minutes later Red and Indian came out the door picking straw from their clothes and hair. The first thing Red and Indian did, after reaching the fresh air, was roll themselves a smoke. It was only after Indian had his smoke going before he said good morning to no one in particular. Red didn't say a word and I didn't expect him to until he had his morning coffee. In fact, the most you ever got out of Red, before his coffee, was a glare.

The stable man nodded his head in the direction of the road that ran through town and said, "You boys are in luck. It appears that the cook is not only sober this morning, he's going to open up early."

I took a look down the street and sure enough the man that cooked our food yesterday was unlocking the door to his establishment.

I said, "What say we head on over and have our last morning meal cooked for us before we pack up and ride out."

Indian said, "Sounds like a good idea to me. It may be a long time before we find another place where we can get meals cooked for us."

Red must have thought it was a good idea also, because he was already headed in the direction of the restaurant, and said over his shoulder, "I've never known two men like you two. You spend more goddamn time jawing about what you are going to do. What the hell is the need for talking, when you know there's going to be morning coffee there?" We caught up to Red at about the time he opened up the door to the restaurant.

The cook heard us enter and he stuck his head out of the kitchen area, and said, “Have a seat boys, I’ll have the coffee ready in a few more minutes.”

Red sat at the table with a frown on his face waiting for the coffee to arrive. After the cook brought out a pot of coffee and Red had taken a couple of swallows from his cupful and smacked his lips, he said in a pleasant voice, “We should make good time today. We will be getting an early start and be able to get three or four hours on the trail before it gets too hot.”

It never fails to amaze me, the change that comes over Red, in the morning, after a couple of swallows of his morning coffee.

It wasn’t long after we were served our coffee that the food arrived. All three of us had bacon, eggs, fried potatoes, and bread. The breakfast tasted extra-special this morning because it probably would be a long time before we would see eggs and baked bread again.

After polishing off the food and sitting back and enjoying the last of the coffee, I noticed the three men that had come into the stable last night ride by and I said to none onc in particular, “The three boys that paid us a visit last night just rode by.”

“They sure are up early for someone who was up so late last night,” Indian added.

Then Red said, “Seeing how they were headed in the direction of the stable, maybe we should head on down there and keep an eye on our supplies. There’s something about those boys that makes me uneasy.”

We silently agreed, paid our bill, and headed out the door.

We were about halfway to the stable when the three came out of the stable doors and mounted their horses and rode past us and went down the road heading west.

As they passed us they made a point of not looking our way. Normally in a small town as the one we were in, you would have gotten a nod or a wave as they passed by.

As we put our supplies on the packhorse, I casually asked the stableman, "Did you have any visitors while we were over at the restaurant having our breakfast?"

"Sure did," he answered. "The three men that have been hanging around town came by and wanted to know if my hayloft was being used tonight, which is might bit strange seeing how they have been in town now for a few days, and never asked to stay here before. Another odd thing about them, they didn't have much to say, but they seemed mighty interested in the fact that your gear was still here."

While we were saddling up, we decided that we would head south for five or six miles before we turned west. Then later in the day turn north until we could pick up the road that headed west out of town.

As we left the stable and turned south, we had to ride by the corral out back of the stable and there was Old Pain-in-the-Ass. He walked over to the edge of the corral, stood there and watched us ride by. None of us said anything but I looked back about a quarter-mile down the trail and I could still see him standing there looking at us. I had the strange feeling that he was thinking, "Where the hell are you going with my traveling buddies?"

10

It wasn't until late afternoon when we finally made it back to the road that had led west out of the town. We followed the road for several miles until Indian said that he was sure the three riders from town had not passed by. Hell, we weren't even sure that they were interested in us, but if they had been they were now behind us and wondering what the hell had happened to us. They couldn't be sure if we had even left town and if we had, in what direction we were headed. That would mean they would have to return to town to pick up our trail. With luck, if they had been interested in us, we would have such a lead on them that it might just be enough to discourage them.

We broke camp early the next morning, and kept moving most of the day. The road we were following turned into two tracks then into a seldom-used trail and finally into an animal trail that turned off in the wrong direction. We had to abandon the trail and from this point on we would have to make our own trail into Indian territory. It was a little bit unsettling to me but at the same time very thrilling as I was in the Wild West that I had read and dreamed about since I was a small shaver.

By the time late afternoon rolled round, we were all dog-tired. We had been pushing the horses hard the last two days. I suggested that we call it a day and let the horses rest up during the daylight hours, we could picket the horses farther from camp and let them eat. Then when darkness set in, we would move them close to camp and then they would not only have fresh grass to work on but there would be less chance of them being bothered by wild animals during the night.

Old Red complained about our early stop as he said, "Hell's bells, you youngsters nowadays don't want to put in a full day's travel before you are looking for a place to bed down."

I did notice that Red was the first one to climb down and start removing his saddle before anyone had a chance to say that he was right. He was just as tired as me and Indian but too damn stubborn to admit it.

We were getting into the routine of setting up camp and it didn't take us long to have it ready. While Indian took care of the horses, Red would gather up what wood we would need to get a fire going. I was the cook and chief bottle washer. While they were doing their chores, I would get out what supplies I would need to make our evening meal.

Of course, the first priority was to get the coffee brewing. Once the coffee was done, and if it was still early, we would sit back and have a smoke and sip our coffee.

After the cup of coffee, I sliced some bacon and peeled a couple of potatoes and sliced them up to fry in the bacon grease.

While waiting on the bacon and potatoes to fry, I put a couple cups of flour in the pot that we had purchased at the general store. Next, I added a couple pinches of baking powder and a small amount of water and mixed it all together. The last item I added was a little of the bacon grease from the frying pan. When all the ingredients were mixed together, I rolled the dough into small balls and placed them in the bottom of the stew pot. I then placed the pot near the fire and put the lid in place. Then all I had to do was let the pot heat so that the biscuits would bake. Every so often, I would need to rotate the pot to keep the heat even. If we didn't eat all the biscuits that evening, they would be stored away until the next meal.

Later that evening, after the horses were picketed a little closer to the campsite, we sat around drinking our coffee when Indian decided on making a nature call. When he walked by Red, Red held out his hand with one finger sticking out. He had a look on his face as if he was in great pain and said to Indian as he walked by, "Indian, pull my finger for me, will you. I have a cramp in my finger that is very painful."

I knew what was coming because Red had pulled the old finger trick on me several times when I was a young kid. I don't think Indian was aware of the old finger-pulling trick and the expelling of pent-up gas.

Indian, with a look of concern on his face gave Red's finger a good pull and Red let go of one that he must have been saving up all day for this moment. It was so loud even the horses tensed up and raised their heads and looked over at the camp.

Even with the fact that I knew what was coming, I had to laugh at the surprised look that was on Indian's face.

Red was the one getting the biggest kick out of it as he fell over on his side roaring with laughter with his arms around his belly.

Indian just looked at him in disgust and said, "Crazy goddamn white man. If the day should come when I decide to take scalps, I'll be sure to have yours hanging from my lodge. But don't let it worry you, I'll take it in the dead of night while you are asleep."

Later that evening just before we rolled into our bedrolls, Indian took out his knife and commenced to hone the blade on his sharpening stone. Every so often he would look up at Red and smile. Red didn't pay Indian any mind, but I did notice, later that night, that Red made sure that his bedroll was laid out so that I was located between him and Indian.

11

The next morning, as the sky started to lighten, I climbed out of my bedroll and moved the coffee pot, with the remains of last night's coffee, next to the coals of the fire, so Red could have his morning coffee.

Indian and I had made an agreement a long time ago and that was to leave about a cup of coffee in the coffee pot each night so Red could have coffee in the morning. In that way, Red's sour mood in the morning only lasted until he had his coffee in hand and had the first sip.

On several occasions, just before I climbed into my bedroll I had found the coffee pot empty. When this happened, I would pour in a cup of cold water and let it soak in the coffee grounds over night. Then when morning arrived all I had to do was get out of my bedroll and move the pot onto the hot coals so that Red could pour a cup of coffee when he climbed out of his bedroll. Old Red never seemed to notice that the coffee was a little weak on those particular mornings. In fact, Red didn't seem to care how bad his coffee tasted in the morning just as long as he got a cupful. I've seen him drink coffee in the morning that was so thick that you would have a hard time pouring it from the pot.

This morning there was a couple of cups in the pot and as Red poured his coffee and took his first drink, both Indian and I were surprised by his outburst, as he said, "Well I'll be a no-good son-of-a-bitch!"

Indian and I jumped to our feet with our weapons in hand thinking something was wrong. Looking over at

Red, I saw that he was looking over at the horses. Swinging over that way with my pistol at the ready, I froze in place. All I could get out was, "Well, I'll be gone to hell!"

Then I heard Indian start to laugh as we all stood there looking over at the horses. There in the middle of the horses stood Old Pain-in-the-Ass, eating away at the grass as if he had been with us since we left town.

I walked over to him and patted him on the back and asked him, "What the hell are you doing here?"

Over by the fire with his cup in hand, I heard Red say to Indian, "You know Indian, I think young Dell has finally gone plumb loco. Standing there, asking that goddamn mule questions like he is going to give him the answer, but then that's just like Dell, always with the questions."

I ignored Red and his comments, because I knew that he hadn't had enough coffee this morning to sweeten his sour mood. I wanted to have a closer look at the halter Old Pain-in-the-Ass was wearing and the foot-long lead leather attached. A closer look at the end of the lead leather showed where he had chewed his way through. It didn't take much to figure out that someone had tied him up outside, and God knows that would be a waste of time with Old Pain-in-the-Ass. I took the halter off him and let him get back to eating grass.

When I showed Red and Indian the chewed end of the leather, Red said, "If they come looking for him and find him with us, they may think we stole him and we'll be hung as mule thieves."

"I never heard of anyone getting hung for being a mule thief," I said.

Red said, "It sure would be a sad way for a great old frontiersman like me to end his time here on earth."

“Don’t worry Red ,” Indian said. “I’ll be sure the word gets back to the Indians who sing of your great deeds over the campfires. I can hear them singing now and I know how the song will go. They will sing about the great red-headed scout and Indian fighter who died in shame, hung from a tree for being a low-down mule thief.”

“Damn it Indian, if they come looking for that mule they are sure to hang you right alongside of me.”

“It will never happen that way, Red. All you white men know that an Indian would never lower himself to the level of a mule thief.”

While I was making breakfast, the banter went back and forth between Red and Indian. You could tell they were enjoying themselves. I was pretty sure no one would come this far for a runaway mule. However, just to be on the safe side, I planned to store the halter in our supplies as evidence to show that it had been chewed through and not cut.

Once we were back on the trail things went along smoothly until I started getting the feeling around noon that someone was on our back trail. The last hour or so the three of us had become very silent. After about an hour, I still couldn’t shake the feeling. I glanced over at Indian and he looked back down our trail and then turned to me and nodded. He must have had the same feeling because without a word he turned north and soon disappeared from sight in a ravine.

Red had seen Indian leave the trail but didn’t say a word. I’m sure he had been getting the same feeling and knew what was up.

Red and I continued on until we came to an outcropping of rocks that had a small stream nearby. It was still a little early to stop but the outcropping gave us cover if needed and a good field of fire. We decided that we would make this our night camp and wait for Indian's return.

As the day wore on I started to get a little worried about Indian and I could see that Red was also getting worried but tried hard not to show it. We were much relieved when Indian rode into camp around dust. I took care of his mount for him while Indian headed for the coffee and then told us what he had discovered.

"The three men that we had trouble with the other night at the livery stable are about fifteen miles behind us. From the look of their horses they have been pushing them hard the last few days and the horses are about done in."

"What do you figure those boys are up to?" I asked no one in particular.

Red said, "It's hard to say. They may be just going in the same direction as we are."

"I have a bad feeling about those three," Indian added.

The three of us nodded our heads in agreement.

"Whatever their plans," Indian said, "they will have to decide between now and tomorrow morning. With their horses as bad as they are they won't be able to stay with us for long."

Red said "We could saddle up and ride hard but then we would have to worry about them dogging us. Let's play it by ear. We'll let our fire die down and move back into the shadows. One of us will be on guard throughout the night and if they don't show up by morning, we will move out before light and ride hard all day."

"If they come during the night," Indian said, "I'll cover the left and Red can cover the right."

"And what am I supposed to do?" I asked.

"Why, you will be right up front to ask them what they want," Red answered.

I said, "That sure as hell don't sound like much of a plan to me."

That was about as far as planning went, because Old Pain-in-the-Ass walked right into the campsite and turned so that he was facing east. His ears turned forward, and whatever was out there got his full attention.

Indian, in a quiet voice, said, "I think our friends have been moving faster than I figured. I believe we will be having company very soon, gentlemen." That said he moved back into the dark shadows to my left. Red followed suit and moved in the shadows to the right of me and that left me out front to meet whoever was out there.

I thought to myself, *Goddamn it, we hadn't voted on Indian's plan and here it was in place. Had there been time, I'm sure I would have vetoed his plan.*

As I sat there, I decided I had better come up with one of my own and I did.

It wasn't much of a plan but it was the best that I could do on short notice. First off you have to understand that I'm left-handed. Most people won't notice right off if you're right- or left-handed. With so many right-handed people in the world, people tend to assume that everyone is right-handed. Hell, I've been around people three or four months before they suddenly realize that I'm a lefty. With that in mind, I turned the holster around on my hip so that it was on my right side. I was far enough from the fire so that I was sure no one would notice that the pistol in the holster was facing the wrong way. Next, I removed my spare pistol from my saddle bags that were lying along side of me and placed it under the blanket on my bedroll. I then picked up my coffee cup in my right hand and sat down next to blanket. I placed my left hand under the blanket and held the pistol in my left hand and waited. I was far enough in the shadows that they would have to come in close to pinpoint my location. I sat there hoping that if it came to a shooting match they would think I was too far out of position to go for my holstered pistol with any speed.

It was nerve-racking, sitting there waiting to see what was going to happen. If they started shooting from the dark, I might be in a whole lot of shit. All I could do was sit and hope Red and Indian had me covered if that should happen.

The wait wasn't as long as it seemed when from the dark someone called out, "Hello the camp," which is the customary call when riding up to someone's camp in the night.

I asked what they wanted and the voice responded, "We saw your fire and smelled your coffee. We been out of coffee for a couple of days and were wondering if we could stop and have a cup."

I answered by saying, "We can spare you that, but come in friendly and keep your hands away from your weapons."

A few minutes later the three stepped out of the shadows on foot and walked up to our low-burning fire. They didn't head for the coffee pot as one would have expected.

The man in the middle of the two others stood there and looked me over good. He had a smart-ass smile on his face seeing me sitting there so casual like with my right knee drawn up and my right arm resting on it with a cup of coffee in my hand.

I could almost read his thoughts. He was probably thinking, *Here sets a damn fool. Three strangers walk up to his camp and he's in a position where it would take him forever to draw his pistol.*

I wonder what he would think if he was aware that in my left hand I had a pistol which was under the blanket, cocked and aimed at his chest. I had already picked him to be my target if the shooting started. The ones on the left and right of him were Red's and Indian's targets so I didn't worry about them. I figured if Red or Indian missed their man, I would probably be dead soon after the first shot was fired, so I put the other two out of my mind and only kept my eye on the man in the center. Besides that he seemed to be the only one doing the talking, so I figured him to be the head man.

After looking me over, the center man said, "What happened to your partners that we saw in town with you the other day?"

"The Indian said he had relatives in the area so he took off to visit them. Said something about being back in a few days. Red's back there in the bush with the backdoor trots. He claims it was due to my cooking but I don't think so. I've been eating the same food and I haven't had a problem."

I saw the man in the center look over to my right and I called out, without taking my eyes off the man in the center. "How are you doing back there, Red ?" and then added, "We have company so why don't you pull up your pants and come on out and say hello."

Red spoke up in a voice that sounded like he was farther away than I knew he was. "Goddamn it Dell, I'm in no condition to see visitors just now. I'm sitting here with my pants down and having cramps like they will never go away. Thanks to you and your damn cooking."

I could see it in the face of the man in the middle that

he felt the time was ready even before the word, "NOW" came out of his mouth and he went for his pistol.

All I had to do was pull the trigger and before he had time to clear leather he was falling backwards, dead.

I heard Red's rifle fire at almost the same time as my shot but heard nothing from the Indian side. Thinking that he may have had a misfire, I rolled onto my side and at the same time took aim at the guy on the left. When I got him lined up, I was able to see I didn't have to rush it. He was standing there with his hands up to his throat trying to stop the flow of blood that was pumping out of his neck, caused by the knife that had been buried there. He was looking at me trying to get words out but nothing was coming out. His pistol had made it out of his holster and was lying on the ground next to him. Now, I've always been a sentimental type of guy so I couldn't just stand by watch him slowly bleed to death, so I shot him in the head. Why Indian couldn't have shot him in the first place and been done with it, I'll never know.

Red and Indian stepped out of the shadows and the three of us stood over the three dead men.

Indian was the first to break the ice by saying, "For a while there Dell, I thought you and Red were going to try talking them to death."

Looking down at the men, Red said, "I suppose we will have to bury them now that we've gone and killed them."

All I could get out was, "I reckon."

"Well one thing is for sure," Indian said, "We don't have to worry about that until morning because they are not going anywhere."

If a stranger were to happen by and listen in our conversation he would have known, by the sound of our voices, that we weren't quite as macho as we were trying to act to one another.

While Indian went out to bring in their horses, Red and I dragged the three out of our campsite. Come morning we would dig a large grave site for them.

When Indian brought the stranger's horses in they were a sad-looking sight. Their heads were hanging and their coats were covered in white from sweating. After removing the saddles, we took them to the stream and washed them down as best we could in the dark then picketed them on some grass. The horses were so wore out that they just stood there with their heads hanging. There was nothing more we could do for them until morning.

The sight of their horses pissed me off to the point where I thought about going over and shooting the three sons-of-bitches one more time but I knew down deep that that was out of the question.

When we returned to camp, I put on a fresh pot of coffee. Normally we would have been in our bedrolls by this time but we were coming down from a high and we needed some quiet time to settle our nerves before crawling into our bedrolls and calling it a day.

12

We rolled out the next morning a little later than normal due to our late evening last night. The sky had already turned from gray to light blue in east.

I checked the coffee pot as soon as I had my boots on. Finding it half-full and still warm, I moved it over on the hot coals from last night's fire. For a change, we were all able to have coffee this morning instead of Red getting the only cup left over from the previous evening.

Due to the number of horses we now had to attend to, I helped Indian take the horses to water and then moved them to fresh patch of grass but that was only after we had had our coffee. When I had checked on the three new horses they seem to be in better shape then they had been last night. I also checked each horse for brands and found nothing. This time when I picketed the three new horses on new grass the only reason they hung their heads was so that they could mow grass.

I returned to the camp and started another pot of coffee and gathered the makings from our supplies to start breakfast. It was after breakfast, while we were sitting back having a smoke, that Red asked, "What do you think we should do with the horses and gear that belong to those boys that are lying over yonder?" as he nodded his head in the direction of the three dead men.

"I've been giving that some thought," I said.

"You always were the thinker, Dell," Red laughed and then added, "What have you in mind?"

"I've checked the horses for brands and identifying

marks and found none. If we turn the horses loose they may make it back to town and people will start wondering what happened to the three riders. I'd be willing to bet that the three didn't tell anyone where they were going or even what direction they were headed. So, if the horses never return to town there will be no questions asked. Being strangers in town they sure as hell wouldn't have told anyone that they were after our supplies and gear. I say we take their horses with us so that there is no chance of them returning to town. We can use them for trade or put them up for sale later."

"What about their gear?" Indian asked.

We thought on it over coffee and decided that their saddles would be something that might be recognized by one of their friends. However, they were too large to drop in the graves with the dead men, so we figured we would take them with us and when we came to good isolated place, we would dump them off.

With our plans in place, we put a rope on Old Pain-in-the-Ass and dragged the three bodies about a hundred yards off the side of our trail and dug their grave. We made the hole big enough to hold all three men. Before putting the men in, we went through their pockets and came up with grand total of three dollars and fifty-two cents. We figured those boys wouldn't need cash where they were going and it seemed like a damn waste to put the money in the grave so we added that to our poke. In their saddlebags there only a few pieces of dried jerky. It became apparent why they were so interested in our supplies—the didn't have shit of their own.

We dropped their saddlebags into the gravesite and then rolled the bodies in their bedrolls before placing them in the grave. Next we took a look at their weapons and decided to take all of them except one rifle that had the letters T.B. burned into the stock. We dropped that one into the grave with the bodies.

After we had the grave filled with dirt, we walked Old Pain-in-the-Ass across it several times and then raked leaves over the site. I figured we had done what was necessary for the three and I started to turn away when Red said, "Dell, you have always been good with words and when I go, I know I would like have someone say a few over me."

I turned back to the gravesite and removed my hat. I stood there with my head downcast, like you see people in church, and said, "Lord, I didn't know these boys by name, but I guess you do, so I don't feel the need to call out their names. I do know that they came determined to rob and steal. They failed in their attempt and for this reason were shot full of holes. Amen."

I noticed Red nodded his head and as he put his hat back on, he said, "That should do real fine, Dell."

Red was always the sentimental one in our group. Whenever he passed by a church or passed by a gravesite, he would get this look on his face and wouldn't swear for the next mile or two. I often wondered if he figured he was too close to God or too close to death to be swearing.

It didn't take us long to saddle up the horses and pack up our gear after we had done our duty at the gravesite. I tied two of the strangers' mounts to my saddle horn and Red tied one to his saddle horn. The three horses only put up a token resistance to being led but I think they were still a little too worn-out to put much of an effort into it and were so happy to just follow along with no load to be carried.

Indian took the lead and moved out in front to scout ahead and look for Indian signs. About four or five miles on the trail we came to a rocky area where we found a spot that was well-hidden and we dropped off the three spare saddles.

We were getting close to where we could run into Indians and if at all possible we were hoping to spot them first. Besides that, we were in need of fresh meat. I think Red and Indian were getting tired of my cooking and were looking forward to venison steak instead of fried bacon and potatoes. Around late afternoon, Indian did ride back in with a fresh kill. At the time we were in an area that had a small stream with a good stand of cottonwood trees alongside. We decided that this would be a good location to spend a couple of days jerking some of the meat Indian had brought in and maybe boil up a pot of venison stew. We knew that our three new mounts could use the additional rest.

13

After two days of sitting around doing nothing but smoking, cussing, and lying to one another, we were ready to move on. I believe the animals were also ready to travel. They were tired of being picketed and had eaten most of the grass that was near the camp site and what they hadn't eaten they had shit on.

Before we moved out, I tied long leads to each of the three new horses and then I tied the leads to Old Pain-in-the-Ass. I figured as long as he had decided to tag along, he may as well earn his way and he didn't seem to mind. I think he figured as long as were turning him loose at night he didn't mind the added daytime job.

Indian led the way and Red followed with Old Pain-in-the-Ass behind him. I brought up the rear of our group and carried a long slender branch and any time one of the new mounts started to pull or hold back on Old Pain-in-the-Ass, I would tickle his ass with the branch. It didn't take them long to learn that where the mule went, they were to follow.

For the next three days things were quiet and we finally made our way into the beginning of the Black Hills. Our goal was to start looking for gold when we reached a river that Red said looked promising. What would make it look promising, I never did figure out and Red never did say.

It was early on the fifth day that we seen our first Indians. Indian had been scouting ahead of our route when he returned and said that there was a small band of Indians ahead and if we continued on we would cut across their route ahead of them.

We decided to hold up and let them pass. Indian explained that there was a small ridge ahead were we could hole up. From the ridge we would be hidden and could watch the Indians as they passed and we wouldn't have to worry about them cutting our trail unless they change directions.

We agreed with Indian that his plan sounded like a damn good idea. Indian led the way and we followed his lead. As soon as we arrived at the edge of the ridge, we secured our horses in a well-wooded area. Knowing that the horses wouldn't get wind of one another due to the ridge between us and the Indians, the three of us scrambled to the top and bellied down in the tall grass so we could watch while the Indians passed by.

Indian pointed to a spot below and to our right where he said the Indians should appear and then pass below and in front of us. We didn't have long to wait as eight Indians on spotted ponies rode out right where Indian had said they would. We hugged the ground and watched them through the tall grass as they passed in single file and then rode out of sight between ridges to our left and disappeared. We continued to lay there for a good ten minutes enjoying the sun on our backs before we returned to our horses.

To allow the Indians ample time to clear the area we took our noon break where we were. It was a cold break without coffee, for fear the smoke of our fire would be seen. We had to settle for water and jerky.

It was while we were sitting there chewing on the jerky when I asked Indian, "Could you tell what tribe they were from, Indian"

"They were Sioux," he answered.

"I didn't see any war paint on them. Do you figure they were a friendly hunting party?"

Red said, "Having spent many years on the frontier, I consider all Indians, in Indian Territory, to be hostile toward the white man and best be avoided if at all possible. No offense intended, Indian."

"None taken Red," Indian said, "I feel the same way."

"Maybe," I said, "we should have made contact with them seeing how we will be spending time in their home range."

Indian shook his head and looked at me as if I was naïve, which I was when it came to Indian's and Red's experience with dealing with wild Indians, and Red added, "Just because they're not in war paint doesn't mean they will be friendly. They could be a war party and will stop and paint their faces when they get closer to their target."

After a short pause Indian added "The Sioux don't like the white man on their land and more so here in the Black Hills. They consider this to be sacred land and don't want any outsiders here. In fact, they don't care for my kind either. It is best to keep clear of them if at all possible."

I mulled that over for a bit and then asked Indian, "You mean they don't like the tribe you come from?"

Indian shook his head and said, "I didn't say anything about them not liking any of my ancestors."

"I thought you implied that when you said they didn't like your kind."

"Goddamn it, Red," Indian asked, "Why in hell can't Dell just leave things be without asking a hundred fool questions?"

Red just laughed and said, "Hell's bells, Dell's been like that since he was a little pecker. He's like a man that has a scab on his hand. He can't leave it alone and has to keep picking at it until it bleeds."

I mulled all that information over for several minutes while I was chewing away on my jerky and then asked what I considered should be my next question. "Indian, you don't know what tribe you are from, do you?"

With a shrug of his shoulders, Indian said, "Not a clue."

"Goddamn it Dell, why can't you leave the man be?" Red asked.

Indian, who was sitting opposite me with a cup of water in one hand and a piece of jerky in the other, laughed and said, "Red, I may have to shoot Dell just to shut him up."

"Can't say that I would hold that against you, Indian," Red answered.

"Damn it guys, it isn't that I'm nosey. It's just since we buried those three men who tried to rob us and I had to say a few words over them, I realized that by not knowing them there wasn't much I could say. For those three it surely didn't bother me none, not having more to say. They were trying to rob us, so I figured they got more than they deserved. But Indian here is my friend and if something should happen to him, God forbid, and I have to say some words over him, I would have to say more than what I did for those three thieves so the Man upstairs would know how much his friends thought about him."

After a few minutes of silence Indian dumped the water from his cup and said, "I'm going to follow the Indians' trail for a spell and make sure they don't double back and cut our trail. We don't need a band of savages coming up on our blind side. If you two head west, I'll catch up with you later tonight or the next day at the latest." Without further words, Indian saddled up and rode out of camp.

A short time later, Red and I broke camp and we also moved out. While we were saddling our horses, I asked Red, "Indian was kind of quiet when he rode out. Do you figure he was upset with me for asking him about his past?"

Red was silent for a minute or two before he said, "I don't know for sure but I don't think so." Then he added with a smile, as he mounted, "If he had been pissed, he probably would have shot you and been done with it. But, he knows you are only a young peckerhead and don't know any better."

"You had better watch who you are calling a young peckerhead, old man," I said happily.

As Red was leading out, I could hear him laugh and say, "If it wasn't so much trouble, I'd climb back down and pull your sorry ass off that horse and kick some ass just to show you I can still do it."

By the time Red was done talking, I was falling in behind Old Pain-in-the-Ass and the extra horses and he was probably too far ahead of me to hear my offer to help him down off his mount. I couldn't help to smile to myself because, knowing Red like I did, he probably could whip my ass. Damn, I loved that old man.

14

Red and I held to a steady but slow pace until a couple hours before sundown when Indian rode in. From his well-lathered horse you could tell that he had ridden the horse hard. While I removed his saddle from his worn-out mount, he told us what he had discovered while tracking the band of Sioux.

Apparently the Sioux we had seen had been a hunting party because after downing two deer they reversed directions and headed back the way they had come.

Indian said, "I continued to follow and in the direction they were traveling they would have to eventually cut across your trail. I wanted to see what they would do when they came upon our trail. When they did come across the trail that you left earlier in the day, they dismounted and studied the ground and had a long talk. When they started to hang their deer meat high in the trees, I figured it was time for me to hightail it back and let you know."

"Do you reckon they will come after us?" said Red.

"I don't see them turning down a prize like this. They will have read the signs and determined that there are only two riders leading a string of horses and they will know it's their hated enemy, the white man. Hell, just being on their sacred land is enough to piss them off and our horses would be like added money in the bank to them."

After scratching his chin for a moment, Red asked Indian, "Will they know that you are with us?"

"I don't see how they could know. I left camp to follow

them before they crossed your trail. They would have to send someone to backtrack your trail to find any evidence that there was another rider with you. I rode wide of your trail to catch up and got ahead of you before I rode in.

Not wanting to be left out of the conversation, I said, "We could saddle up and leave the horses for the Sioux and we could ride like hell."

Red said, as if to humor me, "That might slow them down but sooner or later, we would have to face them. At the moment, they think they have the element of surprise but in actuality, the surprise will be to our advantage."

"I sure would hate to lose all those fine horses," Indian added.

Thinking on it for a moment, I said, "Didn't one of you say something about wild Indians eating mules? God, I would hate to think of someone eating Old Pain-in-the-Ass."

"That goddamn mule would be too tough to eat as fresh meat," Red said, and then added, "About the only thing they could do with that meat, would be to make jerky out of it."

"And then, they would have to be damn hungry," Indian added with a smile.

As Red and Indian were talking, I was getting more pissed off at the Sioux by the minute and vented my frustration out loud. "Goddamn Sioux, I'm for saddling up and riding out and meeting them head-on."

Indian only laughed and said, "I think young Dell here is getting his dander up, Red."

"The young peckerhead doesn't know when to fight and when not to."

I was a little hot under the collar when I looked over at Red and Indian but cooled down quickly when I saw that they both were looking at me with big grins on their damn ugly pusses. Hell, I couldn't stay mad and I couldn't help but smile back. I figured that I had best shut my mouth and listen and learn from the pros.

Red looked over at Indian and asked, "When do you figure they will get here."

"I would think not before late night. They would not travel as hard as I did to get here and I'm sure they will want to keep their horses as fresh as possible in case we were to spot them and try to make a run for it."

Red said, "That probably means that they won't hit us until early tomorrow morning if they think that they have the element of surprise in their favor."

"I agree," Indian said, "but, there's no guarantee. Even though they are not keen on fighting at night, they will not hesitate if they think they have the element of surprise on their side and figure they can get the job done without loss of any braves."

After thinking on it for a short spell, Red said, "I'm for making a stand right here. If we ride on they will see where Indian rode to join us and that will take away one advantage that we have over them. They will only expect two of us and we could set up a little surprise of our own for them."

Nodding his head, Indian added, "This isn't a bad spot to pull off that surprise. We could move the horses over by that rock slide."

Indian pointed to an area about fifty yards on our left. I looked over to where he was pointing and for the first time I noticed the area he was talking about. Long ago there had indeed been a rock slide in the side of a very steep cliff leaving a concave area about forty feet in circumference in the side of the cliff. I could see that when it was roped off it would make a good corral area. Also the cliff itself was too barren and steep to make a good avenue for the Indians to attack.

Red said, "That will work real good for what I figure we can cook up for those damn savages. The hill to our back is too steep for them to come down without our spotting them, so I believe they'll try to hit us head-on in the early hours of the morning. If my figuring is right, we could to set up our camp in the clearing in front of the fallen rocks and make a quick meal. After we have eaten, we'll fix up two bed rolls to make it look like two men sleeping around the fire. Then we move our asses back into the rocks and spread out in front of the horses."

With that, we made coffee and a quick meal, then, using our saddles, saddle blankets, and a few of our supplies, we made what we hoped would look like two men sleeping next to our fire.

It was starting to get dusk so we took up our positions in the rocks. I was to be in the center between Red on my right and Indian on my left. They seem to always put me in between the two of them. I had the feeling that they figured they could keep a better eye on me this way. Before moving off to my right, Red placed a hand on my shoulder and said, "Keep your head down, you little peckerhead."

I smiled back and said, "Don't be worrying about me, old man. You just take care of yourself."

Red wandered off to his position but Indian stayed around for a few minutes as if he might have something to say. To get the conversation going I asked, "What do you think our chances are?"

"If things happen in the way we think, we should be okay. I believe they will hit us early in the morning just when the sky show signs of a new day. If it happens then they will come in fast and loud, thinking they are taking us by surprise. When and if that fails they will come in quiet and try to steal our horses, so after the first attack move back close to the horses."

"God, I hope I do all right when the fighting starts. I've never been in a fight with Indians."

"Don't worry Dell, you will do just fine. We should have a quarter moon most of the night but there is one thing you should do before it get really gets dark and that is to take a good look at the area out in front of you. Try to place the location of each rock and bush in our area of fire in your mind. That way after it gets good and dark you won't mistake a bush or rock to be an Indian and start shooting too soon. The mind can play tricks on you in the dark."

I nodded my head to indicate that I understood, but he still did not move off to his position. After a moment of hesitation he said, "I've been thinking about what you said earlier about not knowing much about me and you were right. I never had close friends until I hooked up with you and Red. I guess that is why I keep so much of my past to myself. You said that I was your friend and if something should happen to me you wanted to be able to tell the man upstairs about me and that I was a good friend. While I was following the Sioux earlier today I got to thinking that if something was to happen to me I would like to have a friend to speak over me.

"Since I've been riding with you and Red, I've heard how you were orphaned as a baby, the same as me. The only difference between us was that you were in a orphanage and I was given a home with two white folks. The two that raised me were very strict but as I look back on it now, they were not any different than any other families in the area.

"Other families around our farm didn't see me as an equal and I could see it in their eyes but they didn't dare say anything because of the man that had taken me in was well-respected and a big man with a hot temper. The kids were different and I had to fight most every kid in the area because of the name-calling.

"When I took one of the old folk's horses, without their permission, I was determined to find my ancestors."

After a short pause in the conversation, I asked, "You said earlier that you didn't find out what tribe you came from so I assume that you didn't have any luck."

"Not a whole lot. I did spend two years with Crow Indians and talked to many of their wise men and received many different answers. Some said that I was Crow but many others said that I had mixed Indian blood and maybe even some white man's blood in me.

"After two years with Crow Indians, I started to miss many things that I had become accustomed to while living with my white family. I no longer had any money in my pockets to buy things that I had taken for granted when I was with the white folks. While with the Crows, I would dream at night of apple pie, the smell of coffee being brewed in the morning, or a piece of that hard candy that the old man would occasionally bring home from the general store while he was in town picking up supplies. Then there were the morning meals of hot cakes, fried bacon and eggs. Hell, I even missed the oatmeal that I used to hate when I was a kid. But most of all, I missed the people that had adopted and raised me.

"After I tired of living with the Crows, I went back to see the white folks that had raised me and to return the horse that I had taken without their permission.

"I wasn't sure if they would want to see me but that was settled as I dismounted from the horse in their front yard. The woman, who had raised me, came running out of the house crying. When she got to me she started hugging and kissing me saying that she had been afraid that she would never see me again. My adopted father came from the barn and shook my hand then gave me a hug. I can still hear what he said to me, "God, son, it's so good to see you all grown and well."

"So," I asked during a short pause, "was it the Crows that gave you your Indian name that neither Red or I can pronounce?"

"Yes, it was and I'll tell you the name that my white folks gave me but I'll have to swear you to secrecy."

"I swear," I said.

"Fredric Bridger Rou."

"Hell," I said, "I heard worse," and I had, but I had read that Frederic Bridger Rou had been a scout and Indian fighter but I didn't say so.

"That is true, but I like being called Indian better than either of my given names."

"After a few more minutes of small talk, the night was getting very dark and Indian said, "I had better get over to my spot and get under cover. Remember, we don't think the Sioux will hit us until early light but we can't depend on it so you will have to stay awake all night. When I hear them, I'll toss a small rock over your way to let you know."

Before parting he said, "Remember what Red said, keep your damn head down," and with that he was gone.

15

After Indian left, the night got very quiet and then clouds started to roll in causing shadows to appear and disappear as the quarter moon moved in and out of the clouds. I was thankful for Indian's advice about taking a good look at my surroundings before it got real dark and placing each boulder and bush in my mind. The shadows had a way of playing tricks on you. A few times there I would think I saw an Indian moving up on me and as I watched, it would turn into a rock or bush that I had placed there before dark.

The first couple of hours, after Indian had gone to his spot, I spent mulling over what he had said about his past. I think he had told me about his past for two reasons. First, he really wanted me to know and the second was to calm me down for the ordeal that was to come.

When the time really started to drag on and the night air had turned chilly, I was thankful I had had enough sense to put on my coat before leaving our camp for the protection of the rocks. Even with the coat, the lack of movement allowed the chill to creep into my bones.

From behind my rock, I could see the remains of our night fire glowing in the dark and I thought how nice it would be to be next to the fire and be able to throw on a couple more logs just so I could watch them burn and feel the heat. Then I would glance over to my bed roll and think it would be even better if it was me under the blankets instead of my saddle and saddle blanket.

Later, to kill time, I tried to remember every kid that

I had known when I was in the orphanage. Other than a few friends, the easiest ones to remember were the damn bullies. Whenever I came up with a new name and face, I would wonder what had become of him. It seemed like every time I found a name for one of the kids another face would pop into my mind and I would rack my brain until I came up with a name that would fit the face. My little game took up a few hours but as the night grew longer and longer it got harder and harder to try and figure out ways to pass the time.

I passed some of that time thinking about how Red had found me alone alongside the road beaten nearly to death and how he had nursed me back to health. God, how I hoped that some day, I would meet up with those four sons-of-bitches who had left me in that ditch. Even finding one of them would give me some satisfaction.

I not only owed my life to Red but everything that I am today to him. He spent hours teaching me what was required to live in the West. When he bought me my first pistol, Red carried it in his saddlebags and would only allow me to handle it when he had me practice. Every time we would stop for the might on some lonely trail, Red would have me practice with the pistol until my fingers would be raw. If I wasn't drawing or shooting, I was taking it apart and cleaning and oiling it.

Then one night after I had cleaned and oiled the pistol and had handed it to Red for storage, he laid the pistol and holster on the blanket between us and said, "Dell, I've taught you all that I can about handling a pistol and you are one of the best that I have seen. However, there is one thing that I can't teach and that is when and where you use it. When you strap on this pistol, it can protect you, feed you, and, if you let it control you and your emotions it can become your worst enemy. Just remember, that when you have no other choice and are required to draw your weapon, make the first shot count and always shoot to kill."

Finally, as I sat there thinking of the past, I noticed that the sky was starting to lose some of its blackness. Soon after that the sky to the east started to show a light gray. It had been a long night but I was proud that I had managed to stay awake throughout the night. I hadn't heard nor had I seen anything during the night and I was starting to think that maybe the Sioux had decided that we weren't worth their time and effort.

My thinking ended when a small rock landed near my hand and jerked me back to reality with a suddenness. I hadn't seen or heard anything but if Indian sensed something, I was willing to accept it as fact.

It wasn't long after the rock that I heard a small morning bird off to my right waking up and giving a morning call. The only problem with the bird call was that it was still too dark and early in the day for those birds to be calling. It had come from my right where Red had taken up his position and I hope he had heard it also and realized that it was a little too early for it. Then I realized Red would have noted the call and was probably sitting out there worrying about me.

Soon after the first bird call, I heard an answering call come from in front of me then another from my left. After that, all was quiet for a few seconds before all hell broke loose. How those Indians could get so close to our campsite without being seen was beyond me. They seemed to rise out of the ground and were standing in the middle of our camp site shooting, screaming, and hollering, I got off one round at the Indian that was in the center and saw him topple over. I heard other shots around me and then as fast as they came they were gone and all was quiet. I looked around for another target but there was none. From my position I could see two Sioux bodies lying on the ground in our campsite. I lay there behind my rock mesmerized by the scene before me.

The next thing I was conscious of was Indian giving my shoulder a little shake and telling me to move further back into the rock and take up a new position near the horses.

After taking up my new position, all was very quiet for several more minutes and then I saw a bush that was out in front of me move ever so slightly. At first I thought that it was caused by a light breeze but then realized there was no breeze this morning. Taking aim, I put three rounds, spread about a foot apart, in the bush and received a low moan from that direction.

I was feeling mighty good about myself when I felt burning sensation on the left cheek of my ass and at the same time I heard a rifle shot coming from the same side. I levered a round into the rifle chamber as I rolled over so that I was facing to my left. When I spotted the location where the shot had come from, I knew that I was going to be too late. A Sioux was standing there and he had his rifle up and pointed right at me. All I could do was clench my teeth and wait for the impact. I knew the end was near when all of a sudden blood appeared on his chest and I heard a shot. As he was hit, he was thrown off-center and his shot went wild. The Sioux dropped from sight within the rocks and I saw Red had been standing about twenty feet in back of where the Sioux had been located.

16

A moment later, Red slid in beside me and asked, "Have you been hit?"

"Just a graze, I think," I said, as I looked over my shoulder in the general area of my bottom side.

Red also took the time to glance down at my back side and said, "I think you took one in your ass, boy."

"Shit," I said and then added, "If you hadn't come along when you did, that damn savage would have finished the job."

"I saw him slip by but I couldn't get a clear shot at him while he was in the rocks. Seeing how he was headed in your direction, I decided to slip on over this way. I heard him fire off a shot but couldn't see him until he stood up to get better aim. When I heard that shot, I was afraid that I might have lost you. Thank God he only got you in the ass."

I would have preferred that he say that I had been hit on the bottom side but held my tongue. Hell, the man had just saved my life.

For the next thirty minutes all was quiet until Indian slid in beside us and said, "Say, Dell, did you know you have been shot in the ass? There isn't a whole lot of blood on your trousers so you can't be hit too badly."

"I told the peckerhead to keep his head down."

"I heard you tell him, Red, and I told him the same before I took up my position. But in all fairness to the kid, we did forget to tell him to keep his ass down also."

"True, true," Red added. "We should know by now

that we have to be very precise when we are explaining things to the kid."

Then it was Indian's turn. "However, it should be understood that when you're told to keep your head down that it should automatically mean you should keep your ass down too."

"You're right, Indian; it should be understood without having to say it. Like if you tell someone to keep his head down he should know that he shouldn't start waving his hand in the air. Are you taking all this in, peckerhead?"

Another five minutes of quiet passed before Indian said, "I'm, going to slip out there and have a look-see." And with that he disappeared in to the rocks.

Another fifteen minutes passed and we didn't hear a thing and we started to get worried for Indian when we heard him say from the outer fringes of the rock, "All's clear, so don't shoot, I'm coming in."

As soon as Indian was back among the rocks, he said, "I spotted the Sioux headed over the ridge in a northeast direction. From what I could make out they were carrying two across their horses and three others looked to be hurt. How bad they were hurt, I couldn't make out, but seeing how they were leaving the fight, I figure one or two had to have been hurt badly."

Red asked the question that I had on my mind and that was, did Indian think we were in the clear?

Indian thought for a moment and then said, "It's hard to say. It all depends on how far they have to go to get reinforcements or how bad they want to get revenge. One can never be too sure which way they will go. Whatever way the situation might go, I think we should haul ass as soon as possible."

I heard Red agree and then added to me, "Boy, I need

you to drop your drawers and get on your belly so I can patch up that ass of yours."

Red headed over to the supplies to get his doctoring kit and, with some embarrassment, I dropped my drawers and lay down with my ass exposed to the world.

After Red had returned, I could see he not only had his doctoring kit, he was also carrying a jug of whiskey back with him. He said, "I was saving this whiskey for when we discovered gold but I figure we could use a good snort about now."

The thought of a good shot of whiskey sounded mighty good to me, as by now my bottom side was starting to hurt and burn at the same time. It was just about at that moment when all I could get out of my mouth was, "Hoooooooooo! Mother of God!" and then all I could do was grit my teeth for several seconds as I had to endure laughter coming from Indian and Red and then listen to Indian tell Red, "You know Red, that is a hell of a waste of good whiskey, pouring it over Dell's ass."

"You have a damn good point there Indian. Here, have yourself a snort."

A moment later I heard Indian say, "Damn that tasted mighty fine."

Then it was Red's turn as I heard him smack his lips, which I'm sure was for my benefit. "It surely is some fine whiskey."

By now I had my breath back and said, "Give me a drink of that whiskey you two lowlife scums of the earth."

Of course my remarks only brought more laughter from the two.

"I don't know if that would be fair to us if you give Dell a drink," I heard Indian say. "He already had his drink poured on his ass."

"Damned if you're not right, Indian. You and I had

better have us another swallow so that we will all start off even when we give him a drink."

With that, I heard them pass the bottle between themselves before it got to me. I tried to get even by taking two swallows from the bottle but laying on my stomach with my head tilted back didn't allow for much of a quantity intake.

While Red was applying a clean cloth patch to my bottom, he and Indian continued with their wise-ass sick jokes at my expense all the while I was in an undignified position.

I heard Indian say, "With the scar he will have on his ass, he's going to have a hard time explaining to the young ladies what a brave Indian fighter he is."

"That's a fact; they are going to think he was wounded while running away from an Indian fight."

"I suppose he could tell the truth and tell the young ladies that he failed to take the advice he received from two famous Indian fighters and that was to keep his ass down."

I figured I had to put my two cents in to save some face even if it didn't amount to a hell of a lot. "Let's keep the story at least true. At no time did either one of you two old farts say anything about keeping my ass down. I do recall something about keeping my head down but that was it."

"I think keeping you your ass down was implied. What do you think Indian?"

"I think it was definitely implied, Red."

Red patted my uninjured cheek which added insult to injury and said, "All done peckerhead, you can get up and pull up your drawers now."

Indian had to put in one lingering shot at my pride,

“It’s about time. I’ve seen about all I can take of Dell’s bare ass.”

“One thing is for sure,” Red said. “Dell and Old Pain-in-the-Ass have something common now. Dell has a pain in his ass and the mule’s name is the same.”

After I was up and had my drawers pulled up, I gave both Red and Indian dirty looks but it didn’t do much good as both Red and Indian were now ignoring me. However, my glaring glances at them seemed to give my pride a small lift.

17

It was Indian that suggested that we should pack up and as he put it, "Get the hell out of here just in case the Indians that we sent packing should return with any friends they may have nearby."

Red agreed and it wasn't long before we were packed and back on the trail. Indian was in the lead, with Red not far behind, leading Old Pain-in-the-Ass. Next came the three horses, who were now trail-broke, and me bringing up the rear carrying a thin branch to be used to tickle the horses' rumps if they should decide to wander off the trail to feed.

I had placed a folded up blanket on my saddle, hoping to make the ride a little easier and it did help for a while but even the blanket seemed to get hard after about an hour. Soon, I was standing on the stirrups trying my best to keep the weight off my bottom.

To add to my misery the sky clouded up and started to spit rain which turned into a downpour within an hour. We cut a stream and Indian led us into the middle and we rode upstream for a good hour. We came to a smaller stream that was flowing into the stream we had been riding in and Indian turned up it and it was a good thing because the stream we had been in was quickly turning into a fast-moving river. We rode up the smaller stream until we came to a place where there were plenty of rocks on banks and we left the stream.

After an hour more of riding in the rain, Indian found us an ideal campsite to hole up in. It was a large outcropping of rocks where years past the base of the outcropping had fallen away, leaving an indent that was six feet deep and a good twenty feet wide. Also, an old downed tree closed off about half of the indent but still left us enough room to camp behind it. Some of the tree branches were inside the indent which would give us a ready supply of dry fire wood.

As I unsaddled my horse, I heard Indian tell Red, "With the tree off to our left, I'm thinking that if we use the outcropping of rock as one side we could use the rope and the trees to make a small corral for the horses."

"Sounds good to me," I heard Red say.

I was only half-listening to Red and Indian while I was breaking off some small dry branches from the fallen tree. I found myself completely exhausted from the ride. My legs were trembling from riding so long with all my weight shifted to them in the stirrups. My bottom felt like I was back at the orphanage and had just received the worst paddling from the wooden paddle that was used at the orphanage to dish out punishment for breaking rules.

I was so exhausted that I hadn't noticed that Red had taken my bedroll and had spread it out in the back side of the indent where it was dry. I became aware of it when Red put his hand on my shoulder and said, "Son, you go over to your bedroll and stretch out while Indian and I take care of setting up camp."

I started to say that I was okay but when Red pulled on my arm and led me over to my bedroll I didn't argue when he said, "Son, you take off those wet clothes and crawl in. I'll change your bandage after we've had some hot coffee and food in us."

As I was taking off my shirt I said, "Please Red, no more whiskey cleaning."

"No more whiskey boy. It's too hard to come by out here to waste it on your backside."

With that, I climbed into my bedroll and lay so that I was on my stomach. It seemed like only a moment had passed when Red gave my shoulder a shake and said, "Here, son, get some of this hot coffee and grub inside you."

I blinked a couple of times and wondered how Red had made the coffee and food so damn fast. After a moment, I realized I must have fallen asleep the moment I closed my eyes.

After I had eaten, Red insisted that he have another look at my wounded ass.

I told him, "I'm sure it is okay. All I needed was the night off that goddamn saddle and I will be good to go in the morning." I sure as hell didn't want his whiskey-on-the ass treatment again.

"Dell, I watched you ride most of the day standing up. We don't want your wound to get infected. If it does, I may have to let Indian shoot you so we don't have to have you as a burden. So, drop your pants and lie down and let me check."

I looked over at Indian to see how he felt about what Red had said and he smiled at me and at the same time said to Red, "Just let me know when you want the job done, Red."

What could I do but drop my pants and lay face down on my bedroll?

While I lay there and Red was removing the bandage I heard him say, "Your wound is looking good, Dell. Hell, you will be all piss and vinegar in a couple of days."

I was happy when he started to put a new bandage on my butt and hadn't said anything to Indian about getting the whiskey from his saddle bags. That was about all I recall about that evening because the next thing I knew the morning sun was up and I don't even remember pulling my bedroll up around me before I was sound asleep.

18

I awoke to the smell of fresh coffee being brewed, and sunlight in my eyes. I was surprised to see Red kneeling next to a small fire made from dry wood, waiting for the coffee to boil. Usually this was either Indian's or my chore. I slipped out of my bedroll and pulled on my boots. I didn't feel the sharp pain on my bottom side but could feel the tightness on one cheek, so I decided that it must have scabbed over during the night.

I didn't say anything to Red because I wasn't sure if he had had his morning coffee but was relieved when he said, "Good morning, boy."

"Morning, Red. I'm sorry that I slept in so late."

"Indian and I felt that you had a long rough day yesterday so we figured rest was in order."

"That coffee sure smells good."

"Grab a cup. The coffee will be done in a couple shakes of a dog's tail.

Looking around the camp, I asked, "Where did Indian disappear to?"

"He's out scouting around to see if our visitors from the other night have returned."

As I poured myself a cup of coffee, Red asked with a chuckle, "How is the sore ass this morning?"

I wanted to come back with a smart-ass answer but know if I did, Red would only enjoy tormenting me more so I said in a calm voice, "Other then being a little stiff, I'm feeling fine."

It was while I was enjoying my coffee when Indian

walked in and squatted down next to the fire and poured himself a cup of Red's coffee and commenced to drink without saying anything. Now old Red could sit there next to Indian and not ask any questions for as long as Indian cared to hold his own counsel but I wasn't built that way and I wanted to hear what Indian had found out while scouting around the campsite. I held my tongue for a good ten minutes before I shook my head and said, "Goddamn it Indian, what in hell did you find out?"

Before answering, I noticed he looked over at Red and both of them smiled. Damn, I thought to myself, those two had been sitting there knowing that I was about to split a gut waiting for any information that Indian may have found. Someday I was going to learn that if we were in any danger, Indian would have put out the fire and told us immediately in which direction the danger lay.

After Red and Indian had had their fun, Indian proceeded to tell us what he had found. "I came across a trail of about five warriors who passed three miles east of us. It was only a few hours old and headed west."

"You reckon they were looking for us?" I asked.

"I don't think so. They had been moving fast and in a straight line, so I don't think they were searching for us. They must have known where they were headed."

After drinking about half of his cup, Indian added, "I think it would be wise to lay low for a day or two and let things settle down."

Red nodded his head and said, "I agree and this is as good a spot as any. We'll be out of the weather and there is good grass for the horses for a couple more days."

I didn't say anything but I was happy about the decision. Just the thought of not sitting in a saddle for a couple of days made my back end feel a whole lot better.

It was later that afternoon when we heard rifle shots that seemed to be coming from somewhere west of our location. From the sound of the shots it had to be some distance away but it was hard to tell because sound echoes back and forth in the valleys. The shooting didn't last long and the afternoon became quiet once again.

I looked over to Red and asked, "What do you reckon we should do?"

"It sounds to me that if it was a fight it's all over now. I think we had better stay put and go with our plan to hole up here for a couple of days."

I glanced over at Indian and he nodded his head and said "I agree with Red."

The next couple of days were pretty laid-back and quiet. We ran out of fresh meat and were down to jerky to add flavor to our soup of dry supplies, which we still had a good supply of. The last couple of days our main meal consisted of beans and jerky. About all we could do without fresh meat was throw a little jerky and some berries I found nearby into the pot with the beans to add a little flavor.

On the second day of our stay, I was able to snare two rabbits at the berry patch and I fried them up for supper that night. Since we had been eating only beans for a few days we all agreed that supper that night was mighty fine.

As we had eaten the meat from the bones of the rabbit, we dropped the bare bones into our bean pot along with the ribs of the rabbit, which held very little meat. After the meal of fried rabbit, I added water to the pot and a couple more hands full of dried beans. Satisfied with my work, I placed the bean pot on hot coals close to the fire so that they would simmer through most of the night. Hell, if you don't have meat for your pot, bones will work just fine for making soup—in this case, bean soup.

19

After the third day in our temporary camp, we were already to move out. Indian's daily scouting trips hadn't turned up any fresh Indian signs so we felt comfortable about leaving but we stayed cautious and alert as we traveled further west.

Around noon we spotted a large number of ravens circulating above the trees northwest of our present location. Knowing that could mean trouble, we pulled up in a cluster of trees for a short conference on what we should do, if anything. In the end it was decided that Indian and Red would scout ahead and I was to stay with the horses. I wasn't crazy about the idea of staying behind but only put up a token argument. Hell someone had to stay with the horses and I was the logical one due to my lack of frontier experience.

Before leaving for a look-see, Red and Indian decided that Indian should circle around and come in from the back side and Red should take a direct route in. After they had a quiet look-see, they would return to the horses and hold a powwow and then decide what to do.

Red and Indian were gone only for about an hour before they returned and I listened in as Red and Indian conversed.

Red, while scratching the whiskers on his chin, was the first to speak up. "Looks to me like a small group of white men were attacked by Indians."

"I figured about three white men were killed," Indian

added. "And they were more than likely hit by that band of warriors that I had spotted a couple of days back."

"You're probably right. From the direction I approached their camp, I could tell the Indians had come in from the east and when they were finished, they headed southeast."

"The white men had to be real greenhorns to make their camp out in the open like they did and by the ashes of their fire they must have had a good-size fire going," Indian said and then added, "Those Goddamn savages did a real number on those folks."

I didn't know what Indian meant by doing a number on the folks but I could see Red nodding his head in agreement.

After Red and Indian had stopped talking, I asked, "You reckon we should go in and bury the dead?"

"I reckon we should, Dell." I could tell from Red's face, as he answered me, that he wasn't looking forward to the ordeal.

As we were tightening the cinches on our saddles, Red came over to me and said, "Son, you're going to have to harden yourself for what you're going to see when we get to their camp site. Try not to think of them as people."

Even with Red's warning, I wasn't prepared for the carnage that we found when we arrived at the clearing. One look and I had to retreat to the tree line and heave up what I had eaten that morning. The remains of three males were scattered about the clearing. The heads and limbs had been hacked off. The bodies had been cut open and the innards pulled out and thrown aside. You could see that small animals and maggots had started to do their work on the remains.

There was no way to identify them, as all their gear had been taken, including their clothes and boots. Their faces had been cut and hacked so even if you had known the men they would have been unrecognizable.

Once I had my stomach under control, I returned to the clearing. Red had removed our shovels from our gear and was talking to Indian. They looked up when I returned and Indian asked, "You okay, Dell?"

All I could do was nod my head. I was afraid that if I tried to talk I might start throwing up again.

Red said, "Indian is going to scout around and try to determine if they took any hostages and, if you are up to it, Dell, you and I can dig those poor souls a place to rest."

As I took one of the shovels, Red added, "I figure right in the middle of the clearing would be a good as spot as any."

While we were digging, I asked Red about something that was heavy on my mind. "Do you think the Indians that attacked these men were part of the group that had attacked us and had returned with help thinking these men were us?"

Red didn't say anything for a moment or two and then said, "I suppose that it's possible. It's not something that we will ever know and it's not something we should dwell on. Every man that dares to come out here takes a hell of a chance. Remember we are in Indian territory and they consider this to be their sacred land. To keep it they know that they must drive the white man out."

Thinking on what Red had said, I not only felt sorry for the three men that had died. I also held some sympathy for the Indians who were trying to save their land. I knew the Indians didn't have a chance in hell of saving all their land. I had lived east where it was wall-to-wall with people. A lot of those people didn't care for being crowded and that left only one direction for them to go and that was west. Hell, if you think about it, I'm one of them at this very moment.

When we had dug a hole about three feet deep, Indian returned and Red and I took a breather and listened to Indian's report. "The warriors left with three shoed horses that were lightly loaded. It looks to me that these three had to be greenhorns and packing only what they could carry on their horses."

"That makes sense to me," Red said. "When you add in the facts it appears, by the ashes, they made camp here in the middle of the clearing. It may have given them a sense of security thinking they would see anything that was coming but by having a big fire, it only blinded them when they looked into the dark." I knew that Red was telling me all this as a lesson to remember. Indian would have already understood all of what Red had said.

When Red had finished what he had to say, Indian added, while looking over at me, "Being tenderfoots, they wouldn't know that the Indians have turned the meaning of ambush into a fine art."

I thought to myself, *Dell boy, you are damn lucky you met up with Red and Indian before you got too far west or some strangers would probably be digging a hole for you.*

When we were satisfied that our grave was deep enough to keep the animals from digging up the remains, we came to the hardest job of all and that was to gather up all the scattered body parts and place them in the grave site. Some of the more gory parts we had to use the shovels to pick up and transport to the grave.

The smaller pieces that had been scattered about by small animals we had to leave where they lay. The shadows were starting to grow long when we patted down the earth over the grave. Just before leaving we made a crude cross from some dried branches and drove it into the ground and I said a few words over them.

The cross had been Indian's idea. He said the Indians might return to admire their handiwork and might dig up the grave so they could re-scatter the bones, believing that their enemies would wander the land endlessly looking for their missing body parts. Indian added that in the Indian world they had a lot of respect for the spirits and many Indians would recognize the cross as a symbol of our beliefs and might hesitate about digging it up for fear of angering underworld spirits that could bring hardship to them and their village.

As soon as we had the cross up, we headed out of there. We only had a couple of hours of sunlight left and we all wanted to use that time to be as far away from the clearing as possible.

We didn't get too far before the light started to run out and we made camp. One of the first things we did was make a small fire from dry sticks for coffee. Once we were settled in and the fire was put out we had jerky and coffee for our meal. We also took turns at guard duty that night and I pulled the first watch.

20

During the first tour of my watch, Indian came over with two fresh cups of hot coffee and handed me one and said, "I brewed up a fresh pot of coffee and thought you might like a cup."

Sitting down beside me he said, "I couldn't sleep and Old Red is stretched out and cutting logs so I decided to come out here and have a cup with you."

After taking a sip of my coffee, I said, "Goddamn that tastes good and I'm happy to have the company."

We made small talk for awhile and then our conversation drifted back to what we had seen in the clearing earlier in the day. I asked Indian why the Indians had been so cruel in hacking up their victims that way.

"I'm not sure Dell, but there may be more than one overall reason. Indians believe in afterlife spirits and their enemies may be a problem to them and their people in the spirit world. By dismembering them, they may think they have eliminated that threat. Then it might be something much simpler, like sending a message to the white man to stay off their land."

After thinking about what Indian had said for a few minutes, I said, "You know, I feel mighty sad for the men we buried today, but I can't bring myself to hate the Indians for being what I feel was overly cruel."

Indian nodded his head and said, "That is a good thing Dell. When someone starts hating a whole group for what a few have done and doesn't try to understand the reasoning behind it, it will sour one's mind and soul."

When I was about halfway through my coffee, I asked Indian, "Do you believe in God, Indian?"

Indian laughed and asked, "What the hell brought that up?"

"Well, before you got here, I was thinking about the men I've killed in the last few days, both white men and Indians."

After a moment Indian said, "I believe a man has a right to protect himself, when it boils down to either you or them. Just be glad it was them and not you."

"I am, but I remember when I was back in the orphanage and we would have a different preacher come every Sunday depending who might be in the area at the time. Some of them were all about brimstone and fire but one thing that they would all say was that it was a sin to kill. I remember one time when I was a little shaver one of those preachers made me and few others hell-raisers, like me, come up to the head of the group. Then he had us repeat words after him which I didn't completely understand. When he was finished with us he said we had all been saved from going to hell and from that day forward we couldn't break any of God's rules or our souls would be lost forever."

Indian laughed, and said, "You said you and a few other hell-raisers were called out. Sounds to me like you were set up by the people who ran the orphanage to slow down you ruffians. Did it work?"

I laughed as I said, "I know it slowed me down for a time, but my point is, for about a year after that I was sure it was only a matter of time before I was going to hell. In fact, when I was walking down the halls alone right after being saved, I would keep my eyes glued to the floor in front of me because I expected that at any moment a hole was going to open up and I would fall into hell. Now, I have to wonder if those preachers were right. I'm not proud of the men I have killed but I did know it was either them or me. Hell, I've killed three or four people, if you consider the Indians that I'm not sure were dead or just wounded, but if that preacher was right, I'm sure on my way to hell."

After a short silence, I continued, "When I got out of the orphanage and was living on my own in New York, I would go to church on Sunday during the winter months, more often than not because it would be warm there, and it seemed to me that they did more preaching about their building funds than anything else when I knew for a fact that there were a lot of kids out there who were hungry and could have put the money to better use than building a bigger church. It made me question a lot of things that they told me when I was a kid."

A lot of what I had said I believe were just ideas that had been floating around in my head and my way of putting them together was to speak them out loud so I was kind of surprised when Indian told me about his experience with religion. "I was brought up, by the folks that raised me, to be a Christian but a lot different than you were. We only went to church when there weren't any crops that we had to get in or be attended to. Then when I lived with the Crows they had a whole new set of beliefs. There were good and bad spirits, even the animals that we killed for food had spirits and we had to apologize to the animals after the kill and explain that we were sorry for the kill but that we needed the meat to feed our families. Mother Earth was the big thing and all things had come from her, so they believe that all people and animals were all related in one way or another. But in the end it seems that all religions have one thing in common and that there is something after death. To me, if there is a

God, he has to be a good God or why would he go through all the trouble of putting us and everything there is, here on earth. I figure if there is something after death, we will be happy. If there is nothing after death, then I don't think we will care one way or another."

Thinking on what Indian had said, I added, "It sure gives a man something to think on when he has nothing to else to worry about."

"I agree Dell, but only as long as a person doesn't let it eat away at his brain."

A short time later Indian said, "I have the late watch, so I had better go slide into my bedroll and get some shuteye. Oh, by the way, I almost forgot to tell you why I came out here in the first place."

"What's that?" I asked.

"Keep your ass down."

Before I could come up with a good answer, Indian had faded into the shadows.

Seeing how I had spent a good part of my watch with Indian, I let Red sleep in an hour longer.

When I woke Red up for his watch, all I got for letting him sleep in was, "You young peckerhead, don't you know how to tell time?" But his mood quickly changed when I told him I had raked up some hot coals from last night's fire and the coffee was warm. For that I got a "Good boy," as I crawled into my bedroll.

21

The next day, after Old Pain-in-the-Ass returned to camp from his night of wandering, our caravan started out with me once again bringing up the rear with my tickling stick. We no longer had to tie the horses to Old Pain-in-the-Ass. They were now well trail-broke and I think they would follow Old Pain-in-the-Ass into the fires of hell if he led the way. My job now with the tickling stick was just to remind them not to stop for a mouthful of grass until it was break time.

Indian scouted well ahead us and around noon we heard a rifle shot coming from somewhere ahead of us. Red moved out fast in that direction and I followed close behind. It was a worrisome time until we came upon Indian skinning out a young doe. After living on short rations for the last couple of days the thought of fresh meat made my mouth water.

While Red kept the horses together, Indian and I made short work of butchering the deer. We didn't know if any Indians were about and may have heard the single rifle shot, but we didn't want to hang around any longer than we had to. We loaded the meat between the three of us and then made tracks. We rode hard for the next three hours with Indian leading the way. He picked our route with care so that if anyone was to track us they would surely have to work hard following us.

When we came to a thick stand of pine trees later in the day we called a halt and built a fire. We gathered up dry wood and built our fire under the pines. The dry wood gave off less smoke and what little smoke there was would soon dissipate as it made its way through the pine branches.

It didn't take us long to cut big steaks from the deer meat and have them in the pan cooking. We also cut off a big roast and put it in the stew pot along with water and beans so that it would cook overnight. While we waited for our steaks to cook, we cut thin strips of meat and hung them near the fire to dry.

As soon as the steaks were done to our liking, we made short work of them and each of us cut a second steak and placed it in the frying pan to cook. By the time I got the second steak down, my stomach felt like it was going to pop. I had to undo the top two buttons on my pants.

After that meal, I sat down with my back to a big pine as I sipped on my coffee and said to no one in particular, "Damn, that was one fine meal." With nods from my companions, I could tell no one disagreed with me.

We let the fire die down and then moved the meat we were drying closer to the hot coals and then made a fresh pot of coffee and positioned the pot close to the coals so that it would stay warm during our turns at guard duty.

After fresh coffee in the morning we moved on. The meat we were drying wasn't completely dry but would keep unto our next stop for additional drying.

Around noon, Indian rode in from scouting and said there was a small troop of about forty-five mounted soldiers located five miles from our location. After talking it over, we decided to ride over to have a look and maybe pay our respects.

When we located the troops they were just setting up their campsite for the night. We watched them from a hill that overlooked their campsite for about thirty minutes before Red said, "Boys, I think you two should stay put and I'll ride in and make our presence known. If all is clear, I'll give you a signal to come on in."

We moved the horses back into the tree line and then Indian and I moved to a location where we could keep an eye on the camp and not been seen by the soldiers.

After Red had ridden off, I asked Indian, "Why didn't we all ride in?"

"We are in Indian Territory and by the treaty signed by the government and the Indians, the soldiers were supposed to escort us off the Indian Territory."

"I don't understand. Why in hell would Red ride down there knowing that?"

"Because it's all up to the officer in charge down there if he wants to escort us civilians out of the Indian Territory or let us go our way. Some officers will welcome you here so that we will stir up the Indians. If they are career soldiers, they know the only way they will make rank is if there is fighting going on. Others just don't want to be bothered with civilians mixing with their troops. Then there are still a few who will go by the letter of the treaty and make us ride back to the fort with them to get you out of the territory."

"What's going to happen if they make Red stay with them?"

"If that's the case, Red won't give us the all clear signal and then it will be up to us to find a way to get him clear."

We watched Red as he stayed out in the open as he rode down to the soldiers' camp. When he reached the outer perimeter of the camp, a guard walked out from the shade of a tree and Red held up and spoke to him. After a moment, the guard pointed to the center of the camp and Red rode on in and dismounted in front of large tent with another guard at the tent opening and Red had a few words with him.

The guard left Red standing in front of the tent while he entered. A short moment later an officer came and started pumping Red's hand and then they both entered the tent while the guard held the flap open.

"I'll be damned!" I heard Indian say.

"What is it?" I asked, with a little alarm in my voice.

"Either Red knows that officer or that is one friendly fellow. Most of the officers I've met while scouting for the army, weren't what you would call overly friendly to anyone they considered below their rank."

We waited in the tree line for fifteen tense minutes before Red, the officer, and a sergeant exited the tent. The soldier that had been standing guard outside the tent flap followed the three, staying a few steps behind the group.

I felt a sense of relief when they walked to the perimeter of the camp where the guard was stationed and then Red removed his hat and waved us in.

With Red's signal that all was okay, Indian and I gathered up the horses and rode into the camp.

When we reached Red and the soldiers, Indian and I dismounted and Red said, "Boys, I want you to meet an old friend of mine, Captain Jacobson." We shook hands all around and then the Captain turned to the sergeant and said, "Have some of the men attend to these gentlemen's horses and then meet us in my quarters for coffee."

With a, "Yes sir," the sergeant turned and named off three soldiers that were nearby and started to give them orders as the rest of us headed for the Captain's tent. The soldier that had been standing at the opening of the Captain's tent continued to follow a few paces behind. I was to learn later that he was the Captain's orderly, whatever the hell that meant.

As we entered the Captain's tent he turned to the soldier that had been following behind us and said, "Thomson."

"Yes sir."

"Go over to the mess cook and see about a pot of coffee."

The young soldier responded with a "Yes sir" and set off in a hurry to obey his orders.

While we were waiting for the coffee, Captain Jacobson told Indian and me how he and Red had met. Seems he was a young lieutenant just out of school back east and had been sent west. After arriving at his new post, he was put in charge of the Indian and civilian scouts. He claimed he was completely out of his element and probably would have been drummed out of the service if Red hadn't been the head civilian scout at the time and taken the young lieutenant under his wing.

Red said that that was a lot of bullshit. The Captain was a good officer even when he was a snot-nose lieutenant.

After the coffee was served the Captain asked, "I see that you have some extra mounts. You're damn lucky that they haven't been stolen by the Indians."

"They tried their best to get them," Red said. "If it hadn't have been for Indian here spotting them before they could hit us, they probably would have gotten them."

"How did you mange to get around them?"

"We didn't, there were only eight in their party and we knew they were coming so we set up a little surprise welcome party for them. We were able to put down a couple and hit a few more and they decided to call it a day."

"You were lucky to get away alive and well."

"We didn't get completely away unscratched," Red said as he looked over at me and smiled and I thought, *goddamn it, here comes,* as Red continued, "Dell here was wounded."

The Captain looked over at me and said, "We have a good medic with us if you would like him to have a look at your wound."

Of course, Indian, who had been very quiet during the whole conversation decided that this was a good time for him to speak up, "That might be a good thing, Dell, having a professional check you out."

I looked over at the Captain and said, "It was only a scratch, sir. They are just giving me a hard time because I was the only one nicked."

I was happy when the Captain accepted my word and at the same time he changed the subject.

"I've lost five horses about three days back and have some of my boys riding double. You wouldn't be interested in selling your extra mounts would you?"

Red told the Captain a cock and bull story about how we found the horses several weeks back wandering around in the woods in the Dakota Territory and, rather than leave them for the Indians, we took them with us. I don't know how much of the story the Captain believed but he said that he would still like to buy our extra mounts. He added that he couldn't pay cash but would give us a voucher for the money which would be good at any fort that we came to.

Red looked from Indian to me and, finding no disagreement from us, he turned to the Captain and said, "I believe we can make a deal, Captain."

"I could use your mule also if you could spare him."

Red took a minute and then said, "I'm afraid we are going to need him, Captain."

For a moment there I was worried that Red might sell Old Pain-in-the-Ass and keep the pack horse we had traded Old Pain-in-the-Ass for. I was surprised, after all the time I had cussed out the mule, that there was a soft spot in me for him and the thought of losing him didn't set well with me.

"Besides," Red continued, "the mule and Dell here carry the same name."

"You mean you call the mule Dell also?"

"No, we call him Pain-in-the-Ass," Red answered.

The Captain looked from Red to me with a frown, waiting for an explanation. When none came, he shrugged his shoulders and didn't ask for any more information on the naming of the mule, much to my relief. He probably figured I was just hard to get along with. I was happy to leave it at that. I sure wasn't inclined to tell him Red was referring to the wound on the cheek of my ass.

Shortly after that Indian and I left the tent to allow the Captain and Red talk about old times. We moseyed around the campsite to kill some time until it was supper time, or mess as the soldiers called it. We had been informed by the Captain that we were welcome to take part in their evening meal in his tent.

After wandering the camp for a time, Indian spotted their Indian scouts at the edge of the soldiers' camp and he said they were Crows. He said he was going to talk with them and that he would hook up with me again at mealtime. I got tired of wandering the camp and found myself a shady spot under a big old cottonwood tree and was soon sound asleep and stayed that way until Indian kicked my boot and said it was time to go eat.

While Indian and I ate with the troops, Red ate with the Captain in his tent. The food wasn't bad but by no means great. I've cooked better meals over a campfire.

After we had eaten and moved off by ourselves, I

asked Indian if he thought Red had fared better by being with the Captain.

"Usually, when the soldiers are out in the field, officers eat the same food as their troops but are served on better utensils instead of tin plates like we used."

Indian and I spent the next hour sitting under a tree with our backs to the tree trunk watching the troops taking care of their personal gear or seeing to their horses until Red came out of the Captain's tent and joined us and said, "I have the voucher from the Captain for the horses so I guess we have nothing to hold us here." He then looked at Indian and asked, "When you talked to the Crow scouts, did they say if there were any Sioux out there dogging the soldiers?"

How Red knew that Indian had talked to the scouts, when he was in the Captain's tent and unable to see, I couldn't figure out. I finally decided that seeing how they both had been scouts for the army it was something they would normally do when they were gathering information and if one was unavailable for the task, they knew the other would get the job done.

"There are a few out there; however, the Crow scouts say there are too few to attack the troopers. They are only keeping tabs on the soldiers and if given the opportunity they will make a try at getting a few of the horses which they did on one occasion."

"How do you reckon we should leave the camp without the Sioux knowing that we have slipped away?" was Red's next question.

"I've been thinking on that," Indian said. "I suggest that after it gets good and dark tonight we pack up and slip into the woods on the opposite side from where the soldiers are keeping their horses. Then when we are a hundred yards or so out, we lay low for a few hours until after the soldiers have moved out in the morning."

Nodding his head Red said, "Sounds about right to me. The soldiers will be leaving a lot of tracks around to cover our departure. What do you think Dell?"

I would have gone along with anything those two suggested. However, I also nodded my head and said, "Sounds good to me." It sure made me feel good thinking they were including me in the decision-making.

When it started to get dark, Red went out to the guard that was by the route we planned to use after dark and asked him to watch for us. We sure as hell didn't want the guard shooting us in the dark.

It must have been around midnight when we packed up Old Pain-in-the-Ass and saddled our mounts and moved out. It didn't take us long to find a good stand of trees where we could hide out until after the soldiers were well on their way.

As soon as we had made the horses and Old Pain-in-the-Ass secure, Indian said, "I'll move back to the edge of the soldiers' camp and watch to make sure the Sioux don't pick up our tracks."

Red said, "I'll stick with the horses and keep them saddled just in case we need to make a run for it. If they should spot our trail, fire off a few rounds to slow them down and then come a-running. Dell, why don't you go with Indian. The added firepower may slow them down even more."

I nodded my okay to Red's suggestion. Normally I'm the one who has the job of staying with the horses. I wanted to think Red thought I was up to the task but more than likely he wanted me to learn more and as long as I was with Indian, I would be in good hands. Whatever the reason, I was happy to go.

As Indian and I were leaving, Red added, with a smile, "Dell, this time remember to keep your ass down."

Smiling back at him, I gave him a salute like the ones I seen the soldiers give their Captain.

It was still dark when Indian and I reached the woods that bordered the soldier's camp. We found a good spot that overlooked the camp and we bellied down in some thick brush. It was still better than an hour before sunrise but we could hear the soldiers getting their gear together to break camp.

When the sun broke over the horizon the Crow scouts were the first to leave. It wasn't long after that the soldiers were mounted and the order was given to move out.

"We'll stay here for a spell, Dell, and see if anything happens."

I figured he wanted to see if any of the Sioux would show up and I was right. About twenty minutes after the troops left, two Sioux showed up and rode slowly through the camp area. As I watched them ride by, the hair on the back of my neck stood on end and I was happy when I finally saw them disappear into the trees.

We lay there for an additional ten minutes when I whispered to Indian, "Do you reckon we should head back and tell Red what we seen?"

"Never underestimate the Indians, Dell; they have been at war for hundreds of years against different tribes and also against the white man for the last hundred years. So they don't take many chances. They like to have their scouts out forward just as the soldiers do."

Once again Indian was right. Thirty minutes after the two Sioux scouts had passed by Indian nudged my arm and nodded to right of the camp site. At first I didn't see anything, and then I spotted an Indian ride into the clearing followed by nine well-armed mounted braves.

The sight of them scared the hell out of me but at the same time I had to admit they were fine looking warriors atop their horses with the paint and feathers. They rode as if they were a part of their horses.

I was glad that the soldiers had left tracks all over the place and ours were well mixed in theirs. I don't think we would have had a chance in hell in making it back to Red's position if we were to get in to a running gun battle with that many well-armed warriors.

We continued to lie there quietly in the trees for the next half hour after the main party of Sioux warriors had passed, before Indian touched my arm and motioned that it was time to move back.

I don't think my heart stopped pounding for the next couple of hours.

We didn't waste time in the area and we were soon on our way, traveling in the direction away from the Sioux who were following the soldiers.

For the rest of the day we made good time. Without the extra mounts and the pack horse, my job of bringing up the rear was a hell of a lot easier.

22

After two days of hard travel, we cut a stream where Red said it looked like a good place as any to try our hand at panning for gold and I was excited to be finally here.

My excitement lasted until I got my feet wet in that ungodly cold mountain stream. It only took a few minutes before my feet were numb and I started to wonder what the hell I was getting myself into.

Red, being the only one of us who had ever panned for gold before, took over the job of showing Indian and me how it was done. It looked simple enough watching Red but it proved to be a lot harder than Red made it look. However, I did get excited when Red's second pan full showed a few specks of color and then I was off and running. For the next half hour, I found nothing. And Indian seemed to have picked up the knack of panning a lot faster than I did. It wasn't long after we started that Indian was finding a little color. I was starting to get a little discouraged when I finally spotted my first speck of gold in the ridges of my gold pan that Red had referred to as riffles. I was so damn happy that I had to show Red and Indian my find.

Red took a look, smiled and said, "I guess that now makes it official, we are now all bona fide gold prospectors."

I took my gold panning pan over to a tin can that Red had placed on a large flat rock at the shore's edge, which we were using to store any gold that we found. As I looked into the can I could see what a pitiful small amount of gold the three of us had gathered during the time we had been panning.

It wasn't long after that that Red said, "Boys, I think it's time we move on."

Being the fool that I was, I asked, "Why are we moving on, Red when we are finding gold?" I was happy. Hell; I was finding a few flakes now about every other panful.

Red laughed and said, "Hell's bells, Dell, we could make more money going down south and hooking up with another cattle drive."

I had to admit that Red was right. At the rate we were going it was going to take a week to make a day's pay.

Red went on to say, "We will move upriver and pick a spot to make camp for the night and try our luck there, come morning."

We hadn't really unpacked much of our gear when we had decided to try our hand at panning so all we had to do was repack what little we had removed and we were back on our way within a few minutes We went inland a half-mile or so before we turned to make our way upstream. Indian had said there might be both white men and Indians traveling along the river so it was better that we move inland as we moved up river. Besides, with luck we might pick up some fresh meat.

We were no more the thirty minutes on the trail when Indian dropped a young doe. With Indian and me doing the gutting and skinning, Red kept a watchful eye. We had the doe dressed out and loaded on Old Pain-in-the-Ass in record time. It was times like this that we appreciated Old Pain-in-the-Ass. He never seemed to mind when we put some additional weight on him. We were at a point with Old Pain-in-the-Ass where we no longer bothered to put a lead rope on him. He had turned into a real trail mule. He was just content to be on the move and was willing to follow our lead. He had picked his position in our caravan and that was behind Red and in front of me. Once in a while my horse would try to slip past Old Pain-in-the-Ass and would end up with bites on the ass for her effort. Pain-in-the-Ass knew his location in the group and he wasn't about to let any common-ass horse take his spot in the string.

Later that day we found a spot along the river that would make an ideal camp, with plenty of grass for the stock, so we decided to set up camp there for a day or two.

For the next two days we panned the river for gold. Although we were doing better than at the last spot we tried a day earlier, it still wasn't anything to brag about. It was on the second day that we had company. We had a routine set up where one was always on guard while the two were panning for gold. The one on guard duty would make routine trips around the perimeter of our camp watching for any unexpected guests.

It was during Red's watch when he rode out of the tree line and said, "We are going to have visitors in about ten or fifteen minutes.

As soon as Red said that we were going to have visitors the hair on the back of my head stood on end. My first thought was Indians and I'll be the first to admit that I felt the fear rise in me as Indian and I left the water and picked up our rifles which were close at hand. I asked the question that was foremost in my mind. "Indians?"

Red shook his head and said, "White men."

Indian asked "How many, Red?"

"I didn't stick around to find out. From all the noise they were making I would say at least four or more. I figured it was best to get back here so we could get set."

Red took charge and said, "Dell, why don't you stand

by the trees over yonder so that you can step behind cover if we should have problems. Indian, you take up a position out of sight in the tree line. I'll stay put by these boulders and I'll greet our visitors when they get here."

We didn't have to wait long before we could hear them coming. I was amazed at the amount of noise they were making. Since we had hit Indian territory we only spoke to one another in soft voices and moved away from the river when traveling. Whoever was coming downstream must have felt overly confident that they could handle any situation or were dumber then hell. Personally, I would be inclined to pick dumber then hell. Long before we could see them we could hear steel horseshoes clicking on stones and on top of all that we could hear them laughing, talking, and calling back and forth to one another.

When they finally broke into view, I counted five and they were all young men about my age or a might bit younger. One of the first things I noticed about the riders was how poorly they were armed for being in Indian Territory. Of the five, I could see only three rifles between them and only four carried sidearms. One young fellow didn't appear to have any type of weapon at all.

They were so engrossed in enjoying themselves that they were within twenty feet of Red before they spotted him standing out in plain sight. The young men were so surprised to see Red standing there that they jerked their mounts to a halt causing the horses to dance around out of control for a second or two. When they had their mounts back under control, one of the young men said, "You sure gave us a fright there, mister. We didn't expect to find anyone hereabout."

"Sorry about that," Red said and then asked, "You

boys out looking over the country or doing a little prospecting."

"I reckoned we are doing a little of both sir," one answered. Another added, "But not having much luck with the prospecting."

Red asked, "If you boys want to light for a spell, we would be happy to brew up a pot of coffee and you can join us for a cup. We would offer some grub but we are getting mighty low on supplies."

When Red said "we" the boys got a surprised look on their faces and started to look around and then they spotted me for the first time. A couple nodded in my direction and I waved back.

The one that had been doing most of the talking said, "We done ate about two hours ago so we're not hungry and won't be a burden on your grub, but the coffee sure sounds mighty fine."

Red pointed off to the left and said, "You can tie your horses over yonder and I'll get the coffee brewing."

While the young men tied up their horses, I gathered up some dry wood and fanned the hot coals from our morning meal into flames, as Red filled the pot with water and coffee grounds.

While the coffee was brewing, our visitors crowded around the fire to watch the coffee brew, and made small talk. The most talkative one, who the rest of the crew called Billy, asked "Have you had any luck panning?"

"Just flake gold and very little of that," I answered.

"We have been having about the same luck. We have been working our way downstream and not much to show for our work."

The talkative one looked over at Red and said, "Say oldtimer, if there's only two of you, you may want to tie in with us. We figure the more of us, the better for protection from the Indians."

"There is more than two of us," Red said with a sour look on his face and I figured it was caused by the "old timer" remark from the kid.

When neither Red nor I added any additional information on that subject, the young fellow looked over at our horses which confirmed that there were at least three riding horses but none of the young riders asked about the other rider.

While the coffee was brewing up one of the young men walked down to the stream and started throwing rocks into the water trying to make them skip across the water which wasn't all that strange except for the fact that he left his rifle leaning against the rocks by the fire. I might be new to Indian Territory myself but one thing I did know was that you never go too far from your weapon.

One of the boys over by the coffee asked, "Are you folks from the new town that the prospectors are starting up?"

"Town!" Red said in surprise. "Hell, this is Indian land. The white man has no right being here, let alone starting a town."

"That may be true, sir, but they claim, if the U.S. government won't recognize their town, then they will set up their own laws and govern it themselves."

I asked, "What are they calling their town?"

"Deadwood," one of the boys answered.

"Deadwood!" Red laughed and asked no one in particular, "How in hell did they come up with such a dumbass name as that?"

The youngsters just shrugged their shoulders to Red's question.

It was about this time that Indian stepped out of the

tree line and walked up to the fire and stood there without saying a word with his arms crossed over his chest.

Indian's appearance had happened so fast that the young men sat as if they were frozen in place.

Red pointed his thumb over his shoulder in Indian's direction and said, "That's Indian, he's another member of our party."

Two of the young men nodded and the other three just stared at Indian with a worried look.

Indian looked the young men over for a moment then raised one arm and said, "How."

I had a hard time holding back a smile while Indian was giving what he figured to be his wild Indian impression. I also noticed that the young men were sipping their coffee a might bit faster and there was no more talk about us joining their group.

Before the boys rode off, Red was able to get the directions to where the new town was located.

As I watched the boys ride off, I asked Red, "Do you reckon those boys are going to be okay in Indian Territory?"

"With no experienced guide with them, it's hard to say, Dell. I guess it depends on how fast they learn. We were all green like them at one time or another."

Indian said, "There has been too much traffic and noise here, Red. I think it would be best if we packed up and move out."

Red said, "I agree Indian and I think it would be best if we do it now."

I then added, "Those boys said they have been panning up river from us and didn't find any gold and I'm sure they left a trail that anyone could follow. I'm for heading in a new direction."

Indian nodded and added, "We can ride upstream in

the water for a mile or two then exit the stream on the opposite side and head west until we find a new location and try our luck."

Being old hands at loading our gear by now, which I might add was sure starting to dwindle in quality, we were soon on our way.

We worked our way upstream until Indian found a good spot to cross over and exited the stream on a rock shore line.

As soon as we were in the woods, I felt my muscles between shoulder blades relax. Riding out in the open in Indian territory was not my idea of a good place to be.

23

Once we had made our way across the stream, we headed in a westerly direction, which now seemed natural. Since leaving the cattle drive, we had always been moving in a westerly direction. Thinking back on the cattle drive it now seemed to be something that had happened a long time ago.

It was late afternoon when we cut another stream. The stream had a gentle flow at this time of the year but by the looks of the stream's banks you could tell that the stream had been a fast-running river during the spring run-off.

We followed the stream north for a few miles until we found a good spot to make camp and Red said, "This looks as good a spot as any to do a little panning."

It didn't take long to look after the horses' needs, build a fire, and get the stew and coffee pot started.

While Red and Indian sat by the fire waiting for the coffee to brew, I grabbed my gold pan and walked down to the stream to try my luck. I guess you could say the gold fever was starting to get to me because I had forgotten how fast that cold water soaked into my boots and turned my feet numb.

I found a fair-sized rock where the stream's current had deposited a good supply of sand and gravel on the downstream side of the rock. Using my pan, I scooped up about half a panful of sand and gravel and with the pan still under water I started moved the pan in a circular motion and washed out the lighter material as Red had shown me. Taking what was left in the pan, I walked to the edge of the stream where I found a spot where I would have access to the water and keep my feet on dry land. First, I picked out the bigger rocks and dropped those back in the stream. Next, I dipped the pan back in the water and swirled it around while holding the pan slightly tipped. After about the third dip, I spotted a gold nugget about the size of my little finger nail. When I first seen it, I wasn't sure what it was until I moved it around with my finger. When I realized what I found, I almost dropped the pan back in the water. Somehow, I was able to regain my composure and then continued to work my pan. It wasn't long before I could see several smaller nuggets and then in the riffles of my pan there seemed to be hundreds of small flakes of gold.

I could no longer hold back my excitement, so I took my pan up to where Red and Indian were drinking coffee and extended my gold pan out for them to examine.

Indian took a look and said, "I'll be gone to hell!"

Red said, "Holy Mother of God!"

I stood there holding the pan and laughing while Red and Indian did a little jig in front of me.

After the dancing subsided, Red got out the tin can and I dropped my largest gold nugget into the pan and you could hear it hit bottom. As soon as I had deposited all the gold from my pan to the tin, I took a quick glance at the bottom of the can and you could see that I had added more gold from my one panful than we had collected over the last few days.

We forgot about the coffee and food and we all headed for the stream with our gold pans. We worked the stream until dusk and had to quit and call it a day due to the poor light. In the short time we worked the stream we had filled the tin can three-quarters full.

When we returned to our fire it had burned down to the glow of hot coals. The coffee pot that had been sitting close the fire when we all left to pan for gold was still close enough to the coals to be warm and the same was also true of the stew pot.

It was great sitting there with our boots and socks off and our cold feet pointed to the coals, getting warm. You could see steam coming off the socks that had been left to dry on rocks close to the hot coals. I figured the socks would dry out but the boots would still be wet when we next put them on in the morning.

We had eaten our stew which due to our lack of supplies was more meat than anything else. We were just content to be sitting by the fire enjoying our coffee and smoking.

As we sat there Old Pain-in-the-Ass wandered into camp. Seeing how he was given free range he was allowed to come and go as he saw fit and he would wander into camp every few hours. As I watched him it seemed as if he was coming to check on the horses that we had staked out on the grass. He would move in among them and nibble a little of the grass and then when he seemed to see that everything was as it should be, he would head back into the woods and disappear from sight.

I happened to glance over at Red and Indian just before Old Pain-in-the-Ass disappeared back into the tree line and I wasn't surprised by the tenderness that was on their faces as they watched the mule. I knew that the mule might still be named Old Pain-in-the-Ass but he was no longer a pain in the ass as far as our outfit was concerned.

I had the first watch tonight, and as I pulled on my still damp but warm socks, I knew they wouldn't stay that way for long because when I pulled on my boots they were still wet and cold.

I was happy that I pulled first watch tonight because I was still keyed up about our good luck at prospecting today and was looking forward to tomorrow's prospecting. The gold fever had hit me hard.

24

The next morning we were all up before sunrise. The coffee had been made and the last of last night's stew eaten before the night sky had started to lighten. I believe I wasn't the only one who had the gold fever.

Red had taken a small deerskin bag from our supply pack and we carefully poured our gold from the tin can into the bag and then returned the bag back into the pack. As soon as it was daylight, all three of us headed for the stream with our pans and the tin cans to start the day's work.

We all found small nuggets that day with Indian claiming the largest nugget and beating out my little finger-nail-size nugget with one that was double the size. After a couple of hours' work, we had filled the tin can to the brim. When I held the can and poured the gold into the sack while Red held it open, I was surprised at the weight of the can.

By late afternoon, we not only had a deerskin bag full but also the tin can and we called it a day. I think we were all happy to call it day. Being in a bent-over position all day panning for gold had taken its toll on our backs.

When we had got our backs stretched out so that we could walk around without being bent over, Indian decided to scout around and at the same time pick up some fresh meat. I thought that was a great idea as the meat from our last kill was starting to smell a little rancid.

While Indian was out scouting the area, Red and I

were busy making deerskin bags from a supply of skins that we had in our pack.

I was on my second bag when Indian rode in with a big old turkey tied to his saddle horn. Seeing how Indian had shot the turkey and Red was much better than me with the leatherwork, I got the job of dressing out the turkey.

Now if you have never pulled feathers and gutted a chicken or turkey it is hard to explain that it is a dirty stinking job. The good part was the thought that we would have a welcome change from our diet of venison. After the cleaning job was done, I split the turkey in half and placed one half in the stew pot with fresh water from the stream and set the pot next to the fire so that it could boil away. Tomorrow I would add beans and rice to the pot for turkey soup. The other half of the turkey, I cut into pieces to be fried up for supper tonight.

While we were sitting around the fire telling one another what a fine meal that turkey had been, Red said, "You know boys, we have been very slack on our chores today."

Indian nodded his head in agreement but I didn't have a clue as to what Red as driving at so I did what Red had always told me, "Son, there is no such thing as a dumb question there are only dumb people who don't ask." So I asked, "What do you mean Red?"

"Today we all panned for gold which left us vulnerable to a surprise attack from white men or Indians. Also the horses should be moved at least a couple of times a day to fresh grass."

"What do you suggest?" Indian asked.

"I think we should have only two men panning and one man on shore to keep watch and cover us if required.

We can draw straws to see how we are to work the rotation if everyone agrees."

"Sounds like good idea to me," Indian said.

Red looked over at me and I said, "It would be nice to know that we could step out of that cold water once in a while and that we had hot coffee brewing."

Indian pulled the first day, Red the second day and I pulled the shortest straw and got the third day. At first this made me very happy because this allowed me more time to pan for gold for the next two days. However, when it was my turn to take over the shore duties, I was looking forward to it. The thought of walking around upright instead of bent over a gold pan in icy water, even if it was only for one day, sure did sound good. I had forgotten how good it was to have dry socks and boots.

For the next two weeks we kept up the same work routine. We slowly moved upriver as we panned an area clean of gold. In this way every few days we would move our campsite.

As we moved up river, the gold nuggets we found were rougher in shape than the ones we had found earlier downriver. Red said this was a good sign that we were getting closer to the source of the gold deposit.

I asked, "Why do you say that, Red?"

Red said, "The longer they have been in the stream the more the constant river action will smooth out the rough edges."

We eventually came to a spot in the river where the bank had washed out a few years back and it was at this location where we found most of our gold.

When we got that area well panned out and moved up river past the washed-out area, the gold in our pans became flake gold and that became very scarce. However, before the gold started to get scarce, we had filled six of the deerskin bags that Red and I had made full of gold.

Our supplies were all but gone and we were down to just a deer meat diet. That evening as we were sitting around the fire eating the last of our meat that Indian had shot, Red said, "Boys, we have about cleaned out the river in this area and I think the next step would be to start mining the area where the bank caved in."

Indian and I nodded our heads. We both more or less went along with whatever Red had to say about our prospecting as he sure hadn't led us astray yet. Red continued when we showed no sign of interrupting him. "I think it is time we gave some thought about how we should replenish our supplies and besides that, we are goddamn near out of coffee."

I had to agree with Red about our dwindling supply but the lack of coffee was worrisome. Not only would Indian and me would miss it but Red going without his morning cup of coffee would make him impossible to live with.

Red continued, "If we replenish our supplies before we start mining the caved-in bank area, we will be able to leave without showing any signs that we have been prospecting in this area. In fact, after a few days and a good rain it will be hard to tell that we passed through here. If we decided to start mining that river bank now and we do find more gold we won't be able to leave. We will have to stay put and protect our claim."

"Where do you reckon we should go to get supplies, Red," I asked as I was thinking about the long ride back to civilization.

"I suggest that tomorrow morning we head on over to that place the miners are calling Deadwood and see what we can gather up for supplies there. I hate like hell to leave when we have found such a sweet spot, but we definitely do need supplies to maintain a long stay."

We fell silent for a spell and then Indian said, "I could really go for a good restaurant meal. Dell's cooking isn't all that bad but some sweet greens and homemade bread would be mighty fine, not to mention a good apple pie."

Red added, "Goddamn it, I could go for a couple of shots of whiskey."

I added, "I hope they have a bathhouse in Deadwood. I think I could spend all day in a hot tub of water."

"Hell," Red said with a chuckle, "I don't see why we can't do all those things. We're not what you would call poor folks any longer."

"My God," I said. "It's going to be nice to see how the other half lives."

25

The next morning we were packed up after having a few pieces of jerky with our morning coffee. The sky was still gray when we headed in the direction that the young fellows who had visited our camp a few weeks back, had told us that Deadwood was located. We had a fair idea where the miners' camp would be from their description.

Once again we were on the trail and we all fell into our perspective positions, which included Old Pain-in-the-Ass. Indian was out front with me bringing up the ass end of our group. I didn't mind my position and in fact I enjoyed it. The monotony of the trail was broken by the fact that about every hour or so one of my horses, being on the young side, felt that he should move up in the string and would try to slip past the mule. All he ever earned for his effort was a kick or bite. I would laugh and tell the horse, "You damned fool. When are you going to learn, that the mule is never going to give up his position in line."

After two hours on the trail, we pulled up at a small creek to let the horses have a drink and a breather. After the short break, we were about ready to move out, and Indian said, "I'm going to scout around a bit and also see if I can get us some fresh meat."

Red nodded and said, "God knows we could use it."

I didn't say anything but the idea made my mouth water. I also remembered that this morning, I had to make a new notch in my belt and it wasn't to make my pants fit any looser. Jerky was okay, if you didn't have to eat it for too long a period, and that was about all we had to chew on for the last two days.

Indian rode off and Red and I continued in the direction we figured Deadwood would be located.

It was only about an hour after leaving that Indian returned without a fresh kill which was unusual for Indian when he went out for meat. He rode up to Red and then waved me forward. I moved on up, expecting trouble. My first thought was Indian trouble. We'd been too damn lucky the last few weeks and when things go too smooth there is bound to be trouble somewhere ahead. I just didn't want it to be Indian trouble.

When I was up even with Red and Indian, I heard Indian tell Red, "There is someone about a mile behind us."

"You reckon it's an Indian?" Red asked in a calm voice.

"No, I'm sure it's a white man."

I was relieved to hear that it wasn't an Indian but that didn't mean we were out of trouble. "Did you get a look at him?" I asked in a voice that wasn't as calm as Red's.

"No, I only heard one man and I think he is afoot."

"How do you know it was a white man?" was my next question.

"Because he was making too much damn noise to be an Indian," Indian said and then added, "Now that I think on it, he must be a damn greenhorn to be making all that noise and being afoot in Indian country."

Red scratched his unshaven chin and said, "Shit, if he was on horseback we could just ignore him, but being afoot we are going to have to check him out. He probably needs help."

With Indian leading the way, we reversed direction. It wasn't long before we understood what Indian meant when he had said that it couldn't be an Indian. We could hear the individual, crashing through the underbrush. About the time we figured out what direction he was headed, we came to a small clearing where we held up in the wooded edge and waited for the individual to come to us.

When a white man broke out into the clearing, I was surprised to see it was one of the young fellows that we had met several weeks back as we were panning gold at the first stream we had tried our luck. I didn't recall his name but remembered that he was the one that liked to talk a lot. As soon as he broke out into the opening, he dropped to his knees which was about the dumbest thing he could do. If he was going to take a break, he should have stayed in the wooded area.

While we were still in concealment, Red leaned over to me and in a low voice said, "Dell, why don't you ride out and pick him up? As soon as you get him aboard, hightail it back the way we came and then circle around and come back to this location. Indian and I will watch his back trail and see if he is being followed."

Nodding my head, I said, "Will do, and you two old farts take care."

Red said with a smile, "You too, Pain-in-the-Ass number two. If you hear any shots, head for Deadwood and we will try and catch up to you."

"Ya, will do," I said with a smart-ass grin.

Red just shook his head because he knew that if I heard any shooting I would be back posthaste.

I rode out in the clearing and was about ten feet in and the young man was still on his knees and hadn't heard me. I held up at that position and shouted hello over to him. He immediately jumped to his feet at the sound of my voice and for a moment I though he was either going to turn and head back into the woods or pull his pistol and start shooting.

Before he could make up his mind if he was going to shoot or run, I added, "Do you need any help?"

When I asked him if he needed help, he seemed to relax somewhat and stare at me. To help him relax even more, I asked him if he had gotten separated from his friends. When I asked that, he finally recognized me and his hand moved away from his pistol which made me happy because I didn't want to shoot the poor son-of-a-bitch. If he had gone for his weapon, being in the keyed-up condition he was in, I was ready to kill him if that was what it took to save my life.

"Thank God," was all he could get out and then start to walk to me at a fast pace which was almost at a run.

When he reached me he took hold of my pant leg like he was afraid that I might ride off and leave him there. As he was hanging on he said, "You were with the old guy at the river."

Before offering him a hand up, so that we could ride double, I asked, "Where are your friends?" I wanted Red and Indian to hear his answer so that they could act accordingly.

"All dead, we were hit by Indians and I—"

"Tell me about it later," I interrupted him. "Right now we have to get the hell out of here."

He didn't argue as he grabbed the arm I offered and I pulled him up behind me. Turning the horse in the direction that Red, Indian and I had just rode down, I kneed the horse into a fast trot back down the trail. All went well until we reached the point where I turned left to make my circle around and met up with Red and Indian.

I could feel the young man tense up when I turned to my left and then when I started back in the direction that we came, he said, "What the hell are you doing? This is the way we came."

"I know," I answered. "We are going back to meet up with my partners."

"Wouldn't be a hell of a lot smarter to let them catch up to us?"

"Boy," I said, "they are watching our back trail and if they have problem, I want to be with them. Now, will you just be quiet until we get back there?"

When we arrived back to the spot that I had left Red and Indian, I told the young man to slide off the horse. He hesitated and I said, "I need to let the horse rest for a few moments."

When I climbed down, I shook my head and looked over at Red to let him know that the young man could become a problem.

When I moved over to stand next to Red the young man never got far from my horse. I had the feeling that if any problems should suddenly occur he would climb on my horse and try to make a run for it. Indian must have got the same feeling because he moved over to stand next to the young man while I listened to what Red had to say.

"We didn't get any indication that he was followed but I think we should mount up and move out."

I told Red, "He said that his entire party was wiped out by Indians."

"When?" Red asked the kid.

"Two days back, sir."

Red looked at the young man and asked, "Are you sure that they were all dead?"

"I'm sure," the young man answered with conviction.

Red looked at the young man for a moment, and then said, "I guess there is nothing we can do for your friends then. Let's get the hell out of here and we can talk about it later."

The young man didn't put up any disagreement about leaving his friends. In fact he looked downright happy to be moving out.

After I was mounted, he raised an arm for me to pull him aboard. I just looked down at him and shook my head no and said, "You will be riding the mule."

"What! I don't ride on some goddamn mule."

I looked down at him and said, "I guess you could walk if you have a mind to."

He looked up at me with hate in his eyes and I was about ready to climb back down and slap the shit out of him when Red said, "Young man, we have a ways to go to get to Deadwood and we might run into Indians along the way so we need to keep our mounts fresh. Now you can do as Dell said or you can start hotfooting it out of here on you own. If you decide to ride with us, I want you to keep your mouth shut and talk only when I tell you to."

The young man seemed to perk up when Red said we where headed for Deadwood and walked over to Old Pain-in-the-Ass and climbed aboard but not before he gave me one more dirty look.

Before we pulled out, I heard Indian tell Red that he was going to scout around and would meet up with us later in the day. Red nodded his head and I waved to Indian as he rode into the woods. I always get that uneasy feeling whenever we split up and I knew it wouldn't go away until we were all back together.

When we moved out, the young man tried to fall in alongside Red but Old Pain-in-the-Ass would have nothing to do with that. He knew his place was right behind Red and wasn't about to give it up. The young man tried to manhandle the mule but all he got for his effort was a couple of bites on the legs.

I thought to myself, *That away, Pain-in-the-Ass, show him who the boss in this outfit is.* Out loud, I said, "Boy, you had better let him have his way or he will turn your legs into raw meat before we ever get to Deadwood."

Once again, I was the receiver of the look to kill. However, he did give Old Pain-in-the-Ass his head and we were soon on the move. God, I love that mule.

26

A few hours later Indian caught up with us and this time he had a hindquarter of venison tied to his saddle which was going to taste mighty fine, after so much jerky the past few days.

When Indian had met back up with us with the hindquarter, he appeared sitting on his horse on the left side of our trail in the tree line. As we rode by him he give Red the thumbs-up signal and as I rode past, he left the trees and fell in along side me, and said, "I don't think we are being followed but to be on the safe side, I think we should keep going until later in the day."

The young man on Old Pain-in-the-Ass must have heard us talking because he turned his head in my direction and when he saw Indian so close behind him he was so startled that he almost fell off the mule. I was amazed and sure that he hadn't even seen Indian at the side of trail when he rode past within fifteen feet of him.

Indian just looked at him and shook his head as he made his way past the young man and then rode alongside Red for a spell before taking the lead.

Late that afternoon we called it a day. While Red and Indian were taking care of the horses, I asked the young man to gather some wood for a fire while I unpacked the gear and got ready for the evening meal. Again, I was given the look to kill but I didn't mind because I didn't like the son-of-a-bitch either. So far on the trail he hadn't said thank you or please to any of us.

The wood that the young man brought in was so

green that we would have made more smoke than fire. I took one look at the green wood and went out and gathered some dry wood for the fire. I held my tongue because I hadn't told the man that we didn't want to make a lot of smoke and let every Indian in the country know where we are.

Soon, I had the coffee going and a big steak in the frying pan. When it was cooked the way Red liked it, I slapped on a tin late and gave it to Red and received a thank-you. The next steak went to Indian and for a moment I thought the young man was going to say something about me giving the steak to Indian before him but then he clamped his mouth shut. The next steak I did give to the young man. I didn't receive a thank-you but by this time I wasn't expecting one. The last steak I cut off, I fried for myself. I hadn't taken but two bites when the young man looked over at me and said, "That tasted damn good. Would you mind frying me up another steak?"

I stood up and pulled my knife as if I about to comply with his request and said, "Here you can make your own steak." With a quick flick of my wrist, I threw the knife which stuck into the log he was sitting on with a thud, not more than six inches from his leg.

The young man bound up and said, "Son-of-a-bitch! You crazy bastard, you could have hit me in the leg with that knife."

"I wasn't aiming at your leg," I answered.

He just looked at me and didn't know what to make of my answer but I don't think he wanted to ask. After giving me the look I had become accustomed to, he went over to the hindquarter of meat and cut off another steak and commenced to fry it up. I glanced over at Red and Indian and I could see that they were enjoying the evening's entertainment.

When the coffee in the coffee pot and been finished off, the young man said, "You reckon we could make another pot of coffee?"

I didn't trust myself to answer but after a moment Red said, "We only have about enough left to make a potful in the morning and that will have to hold us until we get to Deadwood."

The young man looked at Red and said, "Hell, we should be in Deadwood around noon or a little later. I vote we make that pot of coffee now."

He looked around, waiting for one of us to answer and when no one responded or paid any attention to him he finally realized that no one gave a shit how he voted.

After a long silence, Red looked over at the young man and said, "Young man, you haven't told us your name. We been together a day plus the fact that you and your partners stopped by our camp several weeks ago. Don't you think it's time you introduced yourself?"

The young man looked at Red and said, "My name is Billy Olson."

"Well now Billy," Red continued, "why don't you tell us what happened back yonder when you lost all your friends?"

I could see Billy tense up and for a moment there I thought he was going to tell Red to go to hell. He looked over at the horses for a moment and I would bet he was thinking about the long walk to Deadwood in the woods by himself if he did not speak up.

He took a deep breath and then started to tell his story. "We were camped beside the river. It was a hot day and the guys decided to go swimming. We were out of meat so I decided to skip the swimming and scout around the area and see if I could make a fresh kill. I didn't find anything near camp and I wandered a mile or so away when I heard the shots coming from our camp. I rushed back to camp but by the time I got there it was all over. I stayed hidden in the trees to see if any of my friends were still alive but I could see that the Indians had killed them all. They gathered up all our equipment and horses and made camp there. As soon as it was full dark and they were asleep, I slipped away and then I ran across you guys two days later."

His story was plausible, but I wasn't buying it. Who would go out for meat to supply a party of five without a horse to carry the meat back to camp? Then you throw in the fact that he was only carrying his sidearm when we met him the woods. I'm not saying you can't put a deer down with a pistol but it sure wasn't the weapon of choice when hunting large game. The fact that he claimed that he had slipped away in the woods in the dark didn't hold a lot of water after hearing him come through the woods this morning. However, it was his story and there was nothing I could say that would help the dead boys.

I don't think Red was buying it either because he asked, "Are you sure all your friends were dead?"

"Goddamn it, I just told you they were all killed by those dirty Indians." Then, remembering that he was in mixed company, he gave Indian a quick glance.

"Take it easy Billy," Red said as he tried to smooth the kid's ruffled feathers. "If that's your story, so be it."

For the rest of the evening, Billy more or less ignored the three of us which was just fine with me. I did wonder how his story would hold up when he got back to Deadwood. If he and his friends had spent any amount of time in Deadwood, people would remember that he rode out with other men and they would get to wondering what had happened to them.

But I thought the hell with him and his story, I had

the third watch tonight so I spread out my bedroll and was sound asleep within minutes.

The next morning, after my watch, I fanned last night's hot coals back to life and got our last pot of coffee going and had some small steaks cooked when I heard Red and Indian start to stir around. When the steaks were done and Billy hadn't moved, I walked over to his bedroll and gave his boot, that was sticking out from under the blanket a light tap with my boot. The only response I received was, "For Christ's sake, let me sleep."

I tapped his boot the second time and said, "If you want to eat before we move out, you had better get your ass up."

He whipped the blankets off in anger and gave me my usual look, which made my day, as he rolled out of the blanket. He probably would have liked to have said more but with a quick look around he could see that we were all up eating and drinking coffee so he clamped his mouth shut.

As soon as we had finished our morning meal and packed our gear we moved out. With our goal of Deadwood not too far off we traveled with high spirits and expectation. I personally was thinking about a bottle of whiskey to sip on and a big old cigar to smoke while I sat in a big hot tub of water soaking off some of the grime I had collected which hadn't been removed by bathing in cold streams or wet downpours.

We did see several people on the trail all headed in the same direction as we were so I assumed they were headed for Deadwood also. Most were pushing their horses to the point of exhaustion and passed us without a word. A few stopped and asked us if we had been prospecting and when we said yes they wanted to know if we had had any luck. When we shook our heads no, as we had agreed on when we had been alone, they lost interest in us and moved on.

The kid asked one of the men that stopped by if he could ride along with him. The stranger looked at the mule and said, “I’m moving fast, boy. Do you think that mule will keep up?”

I spoke up and said, “The mule stays with us, the kid can do whatever he wants.”

The stranger laughed and said, “Hell’s bells kid, my horse is already worn down. I’m sure as hell not going to double up on him.” With that he waved and rode off.

Red said, “Billy, I’m afraid you are going to have to stick with us until we get to Deadwood.”

The kid didn’t say anything but when Red turned and started to move on the kid gave Red the look that I thought he saved only for me.

27

It must have been around noon when we topped a ridge that looked down into the miner's town called Deadwood. We pulled up and sat there for several minutes and looked the place over.

I was stunned and said to no one in particular, "Where in hell did all those people come from?"

Red just laughed and said, "When someone strikes gold, the rush is on."

"Shit," I said, "there must be two or three thousand people down there. All of them sure as hell couldn't have found gold."

"I would make it more than three thousand," Red said, and added, "If only a few of them have hit good paydirt, you haven't seen anything yet. The word about gold being found will move like a wildfire on a windy day and this place will draw people faster than flies to dog shit."

From our position on the ridge, we had a good view of Deadwood. It was more like a tent city than anything else. A few places had one or more log walls but the roofs were mostly canvas-covered. Some of the newer buildings that were under construction looked to be mostly made of wood. There was even some construction going on the side hills of the town.

Running through the center of these establishments was a wet muddy trail wide enough to allow two wagons to pass if they moved carefully.

We kneed our horses off the ridge and headed down

to the town of Deadwood. When we reached the edge of the town, Billy slid off Old Pain-in-the-Ass and walked off toward the center of Deadwood without so much as a thank-you, goodbye, or a wave. I watched him walk through the mud and disappear into the mass of people that seemed like ants on the move. I personally wasn't going to miss the arrogant little bastard.

We slowly made our way down what was the main street of Deadwood with our horses' hoofs making sucking noises in the six-inch-deep mud that covered the street. As we passed each building, I made a mental note of its location and what service it might render. In the town's short history, I counted five saloons, a large part-log/ part-tent establishment with a sign claiming to have private sleeping quarters for rent, another tent that had a sign that stated hot meals were served, and another tent claiming to be a bath house which I made a note of. The remaining tent/log structures claimed to offer one type service or another and many smaller tents appeared to be living quarters or were selling odds and ends out the open end of the tent. Along our way through town we saw two muddy fistfights on the street and heard gunfire coming from somewhere in town.

I'll be the first to admit that the three of us have done our share of cussing but in that short ride through Deadwood, I heard more cuss words used in more ways than I had ever heard in my life. In fact, I heard some that I didn't know existed. I reckon it was due to the number of men present and the lack of homemaking women about. I figured that would soon change as more families made their way to Deadwood.

We finally made our way through the mass of men who all seemed to be in a hurry going or coming from somewhere.

Red pointed out an open spot at the edge of town and said, "What say we pitch camp here? There is plenty of grass on the hillside for our stock."

"What the hell are we going to do with Old Pain-in-the Ass? He won't stay ground-hitched for long and there are too many people around to let him roam free," I voiced.

Indian said, "I spotted a place that had a sign out front that claimed to be a stable. We could stable him there with instructions to keep him in a corral at all times."

We all agreed that would be best. It would probably piss Old Pain-in-the-Ass off but I figured it would have to be that or lose him. With all the people around, he wouldn't wander free long before someone would claim him and then we would have to shoot the sorry son-of-a-bitch who claimed the mule just so that we could get the damn animal back.

After we had our camp set up, we divided our gold into three of our saddle bags so that if something should happen to one of us, such as a robbery, we wouldn't lose all our gold. Deadwood was made up of all kinds of people and we wanted to play it safe. When the three of us were together we didn't feel we would have to worry too much about holding our own. The only time we felt we would be vulnerable was when we were separated from one another and that was bound to happen from time to time.

We put a rope around Old Pain-in-the-Ass's neck, picked up our rifles and saddle bags and headed down the street to where Indian had spotted the stable. It was a hell of a lot harder walking in the street than it had been when we were on horseback. Every step you took you would sink two or three inches into the mud, which was a mixture of horse shit and piss and what was left over from the last rain. Whatever else that was mixed into the goop, I didn't want to think about but I'm sure it was all there. It didn't take us long to discover that the best place to walk was to get as close to the tents as possible, where there was less horse traffic and for this reason less mud.

When we reached the log-walled building with the canvas roof that claimed to be a stable, we walked around it before entering. Out back we found a fenced-in corral. I placed a hand on one of the corner posts to test its strength and found it solid. We continued our tour around the structure until we came to the entrance where we met up with the proprietor and worked out the cost to house Old Pain-in-the-Ass. Not knowing how long our stay would be in Deadwood, we only paid for a couple of days.

"Before we hand the mule over to you," Red said, "there are a few things that you need to know."

The proprietor interrupted Red and said, "Mister, I've been handing animals my whole goddamn life and now you are going to come waltzing in here and tell me how I'm to run my business?"

Red just smiled and said, "No, no, don't get me wrong. I just want to mention that the mule likes to break loose. So don't stake him out on green grass so that you can save money on hay. He can untie any knot or pull up a tie-down stake and if all that fails he will chew his way through the rope. During the day you can put him in the corral but at night you will need to put him in a very secure stanchion.

"If you let the mule get away you are going to piss off Dell and Indian here. You had better hope that Dell catches up with you first. He will just shoot you outright and be done with it, but if the Indian gets to you first, I get the shakes just thinking about what he will do to you."

The proprietor looked over at Indian, who was standing there with his arms crossed and a smile on his face while looking the owner over.

The proprietor quickly made an attitude adjustment and I could see him swallow a couple of times before he said, "No need to worry, gentlemen, I'll keep a good eye on the mule."

With our worries for Old Pain-in-the-Ass taken care of, we went out and stood on the street in front of the stable trying to decide what we wanted to do next. It came down to one of two things, a drink first then food or food first then a drink. Seeing how we had been on a diet of mainly jerky and deer meat for the last couple of days, food first won out.

We stopped the first well-fed man that walked past and Red asked, "Sorry to bother you mister, but where can three powerful hungry men find the best meal in town?"

The gentleman smiled and said, with no hesitation, "There is only one place in Deadwood if you're looking for a good meal and that is at the Grand Central Hotel. The place isn't much to look at but the kitchen is run by Aunt Lou and she serves the best goddamn food in town without question."

The gentleman gave us the directions to the Grand Central Hotel before he moved off into the crowd and disappeared into the moving mass of people.

Following the man's directions, we soon found the Grand Central Hotel, which I assure you didn't even come close to living up to its grand name. However, we were hungry, so we made our way to the area where tables had been set up and found an empty table and sat ourselves down. On each table were several one-page sheets with the menu printed very neatly.

Red, without picking up the menu, looked over at me and asked, "What kind of meat are they serving?"

Glancing at the menu, I said, "They have beef, venison, and pork dinners and they all come with baked or fried potatoes, green beans cooked with bacon, bread, coffee, and apple pie for dessert."

Because of our diet of venison over the last few weeks we all opted for the beefsteak dinner. I think we all had forgotten that only a couple of months back we had taken a vow that we would never eat beef again. Oh my, how soon we forget.

A pot of coffee was placed on our table by the man who took our orders. We all drank our coffee black so we ignored the sugar that was in a bowl on the table. By the time our food had arrived we had consumed all of the coffee and ordered another potful.

The steaks were cooked to perfection with a light pink in the center, and were covered with onions. The potatoes had been fried in bacon fat until crispy around the ends. The string beans had small pieces of bacon mixed in. The bread biscuits that were served with the meal were so fresh that they were still warm and the butter melted as you spread it on the bread. There was some blackberry jelly on the table of which I added a generous supply to each of the biscuits I ate.

The apple pie was excellent and after polishing off a piece of that, Red and I pushed our chairs back and rolled smokes and drank the rest of the coffee. When Indian had taken his first bite of that pie, he gave out a big sigh of pleasure and while Red and I were enjoying our smokes, Indian ordered his second piece of pie.

As we sat there, letting our stomachs settle the food and enjoying our smokes, a black lady came out of the kitchen, stopping at each table to chat with the customers. When she stopped at our table and asked if our food was satisfactory, we all agreed that it was the best meal we had had in a very long time.

I said, "Ma'am, the food was so good that there will be no need to clean the plate because we didn't leave anything behind."

"The boy sure is right, ma'am, and your name must be Aunt Lou," Red said. When Aunt Lou nodded to confirm, he added, "Hell, we heard about your cooking all the way down on the Texas panhandle and made the long ride up here just for the meal."

"My word, my cooking must have spread fast to get all the way to Texas and you boys must have rode hard to get here, seeing how I've only been the kitchen manager here for a short time."

Red had a quick response to that. "That only goes to show just how good your food is. Your good reputation has preceded you here."

Aunt Lou laughed and said to Red, "With that red tint in your hair and that blarney coming out of your mouth, you must have a wee bit of the Irish blood in you."

Aunt Lou left our table and moved on to the next, but before leaving she waved and asked us to come back again soon.

We finished our smokes and downed the last of our coffee and left the Grand Central Hotel and headed for the nearest saloon down the street.

After a couple of drinks, I started thinking about that hot bath that I had been promising myself while still on the trail. Swallowing the last of my drink, I informed Red and Indian that I was ready for that bath and that we could meet up later if they were inclined to have a few more drinks. Both opted for the drinks and I left them there as I headed back to camp for a clean set of clothes.

28

After retrieving my clean clothes, I headed in the direction where I had spotted the bathhouse or maybe I should say bath tent.

As I was walking down the street, heading in the required direction, I spotted Billy coming my way. When we were only a few feet apart, I raised my hand in greeting but before I could say hello, he turned his head away as if he hadn't seen me and passed on by. I shrugged my shoulders and thought to myself, I'll never figure that kid out, but I wasn't going to let that bother me.

When I reached the tent that had the handwritten sign claiming it to be a bathhouse, I didn't hesitate or break stride as I entered. Inside the tent there were five large wooden tubs, or a better description would be large wooden horse troughs. I could see that there was a smaller section in the back of the tent that was partitioned off and a sign that said LADIES ONLY. At the time, I wondered how ladies would get to and from their bath area with the men bathing out front but then I figure there must be an opening in the back of the tent. I was later to find out how wrong I was.

The attendant came over to me and asked, "You looking to use one of the tubs?"

When I told him I was, his next question as, "Do you want clean water or used water." When he saw that I was frowning at him he added, "Used water has been used by someone else and cost less. Clean water will cost you a little more."

I opted for the clean water and then was directed to a bench where I could wait while the water was being heated and made ready for me.

They must have been keeping water warm out back because it wasn't too long before three Chinese men were carrying hot buckets of water and filling one of the tubs.

Alongside each tub was a stool for sitting or for piling your clothes and a tall coat rack where you could hang items.

When the proprietor said my bath was ready, I leaned my rifle against the tub and hung my pistol, with the holster, within hand's reach, on the coat rack. The saddle bags were placed on the stool where I could keep an eye on them.

As I stripped off my dirty clothes, I allowed them to fall on the ground. I figured they couldn't get any dirtier than they already were.

I stepped into the tub and slowly lowered myself into the hot water. When the water was up around my shoulders, I gave out a deep sigh and felt my body relax completely. Taking a deep breath I bent my knees and slid down until my head was under water. After I resurfaced, I picked up the lye soap that was supplied with the price of the bath and went to work removing all the grime from my body. After my scrub-down, I just sat in the water and enjoyed the pleasure of the warm water.

When the water started to cool down, I called the proprietor over and told him go heat up another tub of water for me. He looked at me like I was crazy and said, "You want to take another bath?"

"I sure do," I responded.

Shaking his head like I must be a little touched in the head, he called out to his Chinese workers, "Fill another tub with clean hot water, boys."

I sat in the tub with my dirty water until the proprietor told me that the new tub of water was full and ready. I climbed out and picked up my weapons, gear, and saddle bags and moved to my new location. When I was midway between the two tubs, I heard the proprietor say, "Good afternoon, ladies."

I turned around without thinking to face the tent opening and there stood three ladies. Hell's bells, it all happened so fast that I went into shock and just stood there, bare-assed naked, as the ladies walked past not more than a couple of feet away. The first two ladies paid me no mind but the last one looked me over pretty good and smiled, then said, "Why hello there, sweetie," and then they were past me. As they passed my new tub of clean water, I noticed for the first time, a man sitting in a tub next to my new tubfull, smoking a cigar. As the ladies passed he, he said, "Hello, ladies," and they all responded with smiles and a "Hello Charlie."

When I finally came to my senses, the man in the tub said with a smile, "Don't let the ladies embarrass you, my friend. They have probably seen more naked men than you could count to in two minutes."

Me, I was still too stunned to talk so I just nodded my head and quickly gathered up my gear and moved to my new tub of water.

I slowly lowered myself into the hot water. When my body got used to the hot water, I took a deep breath then slipped even lower until my head was completely under water. I stayed that way as long as I could hold my breath. When I could hold it no longer, I came out from under the water spraying water and drawing in a deep breath of air.

I heard the gentleman next to me laugh as I came out of the water. I must have been a sight coming up and spraying water all around. I looked over at him and had to laugh myself as he said, "You were down so long that I thought for a minute there that I was going to have to get out of my tub so that I could grab you by the hair and pull you up to keep you from drowning, young man."

Feeling that I owed him an explanation I said, "I'm so sick of bathing in cold creeks and rivers I couldn't help indulging myself in the warm water."

"I know the feeling, young fellow. You just get into camp?"

"Yes sir. My partners and I just rode in a few hours ago."

"I've only been here a few days myself. I brought in a load of supplies for sale to the local merchants and, I'm sad to say, a wagonload of prostitutes that were in a powerful hurry to get here. By the way, my name is Charlie Utter."

I told him my name and, after accepting the offer of one of his cigars, we were soon on a first-name basis. We discovered that we were both from the state of New York. He was born near Niagara Falls but had moved to Illinois at an early age.

I was still soaking in the water when Charlie said, "Well, Dell, it has been good talking to you but I have got some business to take care of."

"Good meeting and talking to you too, Charlie. If I should see you again, I'll buy you a drink to pay you back for the fine cigar."

Charlie said, as he waved and headed for the tent opening, "I'll be holding you to that, Dell."

I was still in the water when the three ladies came out from behind their sectioned-off area of the bath tent. The one that had spoken to me earlier smiled at me again and said, as she passed, “Don’t stay in that water too long, cowboy, or you will get waterlogged.”

All I could manage to get out, as I put my hands over my private parts and felt the heat rising in my face again was, “No ma’am.”

29

I stayed in the tub until the water started to cool down. After drying off with a towel that was supplied along with the bath, it felt damn good to be clean and at the same time be able to put on clean clothes. I paid my bath bill and stepped out of bathhouse with my gear and a bundle of dirty clothes.

Standing there for a moment, I watched people pass by. They all seemed to be in a hurry. Finally, I spotted a man who looked to be a down-and-outer wandering down the street. When he reached my position, I stopped him and asked where I could find a place that would clean my clothes. He pointed down the street in the opposite direction I had come from and said, "Down the street is Chinatown and there you will find several places that will clean your clothes for you."

After thanking the fellow, I gave him four bits and I headed in the direction he pointed, and he headed for the nearest saloon, which was across the street.

It didn't take long and I was soon in a part of town that gave me the feeling as if I had just stepped off a boat and into a foreign country.

The smell of food was everywhere. It seemed as if half the businesses along the street were cooking food and selling it. The smell made my mouth water and if I hadn't eaten a couple of hours or so ago, I would have been sampling some of that food. I promised myself that one day soon, I would return to eat my fill.

The first sign that I came to that was written in English claimed to be a cleaners, I entered. It was a small area with a counter by the door with cloth piled on shelves in back of the counter. There was no one at the counter but there was a small bell with a handle sitting on the counter which I picked up and shook. Within moments, an elderly gentleman with stooped shoulders came from the back of the shop and bowed to me. His bowing made me kind of embarrassed so to cover my embarrassment, I bowed back to him as he said, "It is a good day."

"Yes, it is," I said and we bowed again.

"You like to have clothes cleaned, yes?"

"Yes," I said as I pushed my bundle of dirty clothes across the counter.

The old man reached under the counter and took out two pieces of paper with Chinese printing on it and handed one piece to me and said, "You come back tomorrow. Same time. Clothes be all cleaned," and then we bowed to one another.

Taking the slip of paper, I said, "I'll be back tomorrow," and turned to leave. The old man came from around the counter and opened the door for me and once again we bowed to one another.

Out on the street, I had to smile and think to myself, *Now I see why it seems that all Chinese people are slim at the waist. It has to do with all the bowing they do. It might be a good habit to get into seeing how so many of us white-skinned people have big guts hanging over our belts.*

I turned and headed back the way I had come. Suddenly, I came to the end of Chinatown. It was as if someone had drawn a line. I stood there for a moment with one foot in Chinatown and the other foot in what the white man called Deadwood. First, I looked in one direction and then the other. One way was China and the other direction was the white man's world. I nodded my head, thinking, *If both parties could get together I'm sure we could learn many good things from one another.* Not being a deep thinker, I didn't know how this could take place. I said to myself, *What the hell could I do about it other than treat everyone the same while always keeping in mind, that if you screw with me, I'm going to screw you right back, only harder.*

As I stood there considering the problems of the world, I reached up and scratched my several-days-old whiskers and decided that at the moment my biggest problem was the fact that I sure could use a shave.

I headed back in the direction where I had left Red and Indian while checking out all the businesses along the street. One thing was for sure, a person wouldn't have to go far to find a place to drink or dip his wick if he should so desire.

It didn't take long before I came to a tent with a sign nailed to a post out front that claimed you could get a shave and hair cut inside. I entered the tent and found only one man waiting ahead of me so I sat on a bench that was provided for that purpose and waited my turn in the barber's chair.

When the barber nodded to me, I got up and leaned my rifle against the tent wall. I took off my holster and after removing the pistol, placed the holster alongside my rifle. I moved to the barber chair with my pistol and saddlebags in hand and placed them on my lap as the barber covered me with a white cloth.

If he thought my actions were strange, he didn't say. Me, I felt naked without my pistol or rifle close at hand. Maybe it came from living in Indian territory so long, where danger could appear within a moment's notice, and that had made me a wee bit paranoid.

When the barber had me covered he asked, "What will it be, mister, a shave or hair cut or both?"

"A shave for sure and maybe you could trim up the ends of my hair a bit. I don't want it so short that my hat won't fit," I answered.

The barber tried his damndest to get a conversation going while I sat there but after my one-word answers, he finally gave up and let me sit there in peace while he went to work on me.

When the barber was done cutting he asked, "Would you care for a little lavender water sir? It's only a nickel more."

"No, thank you" I said, as I thought about the ration of shit I would have gotten from Red and Indian if I were to show up smelling like a flower. Now, if it had been a young lady I was going to see, I would have said "Hell yes."

Once I was back out in the street, I decided that it was time to rejoin my friends.

30

The first place I stopped to look for them was the saloon where I had left them when I had headed to the bath house. They were no longer there but I decided to belly up to the bar and have a drink. I was about halfway done with my watered-down drink when someone moved up to the bar beside me and said, “Dell, as long as you are here, I’ll be calling you on that drink you promised me.”

Turning in surprise that someone should know my name, I found Charlie Utter standing beside me.

“Hello, Charlie,” I said. “It’s nice to find a friendly face among so many strangers.”

“Being new in town, I know the feeling myself.”

“What are you drinking Charlie?” I asked.

“I’ll have the same as you are having.”

As soon as I caught the bartender’s eye, I ordered two more drinks. After the drinks arrived, we raised our glasses and toasted one another and downed half our drinks.

As we set glasses back down, Charlie fired up one of his cigars and offered me one which I declined in favor of one of my self-rolled smokes. As I was lighting my smoke, a commotion occurred at the door. I turned toward the disturbance to see a fellow standing in the doorway saying, “What the hell kind of place is this. A goddamn saloon or have I walked in on some kind of goddamn wake?” I heard a few chuckles around the room which didn’t seem to bother the fellow as he stepped into the room. Then in a rather high-pitched voice he added, “Well aren’t any of you pansy-assed bastards going to offer to buy this lady a drink?"

I took a closer look at what I had first considered to be a man and realized that what I was looking at was a woman entirely dressed in men's clothing, carrying a rifle over her shoulder and a pistol strapped to her waist.

She looked over our way and said, in a loud voice, "Well I'll be a son-of-a-bitch, is that that no-account Charlie Utter I see bellied up to that god-damn bar?"

Walking up to Charlie she reached out her hand and as they shook hands she said, "You're looking good you old fart."

"You seem to be doing well yourself, Jane."

"Shit Charlie, you know me. I'm always on top of the world but I'd feel a hell of a lot better if I had a goddamn shot of whisky in my hand."

Charlie called the bartender and ordered a double for the woman. She polished it off without stopping for air then, slapping down the glass on the bar, indicated to the bartender that she wanted a refill.

While sipping on her second double she turned to me and said, "Charlie, is this handsome young peckerhead standing beside you a friend of yours?"

"That he is, Jane. Dell, I would like you to meet Calamity Jane, Army scout, nurse, and prospector along with many other trades."

We shook hands and I said, "I'm glad to meet you ma'am."

"You had better start calling me Calamity Jane or I may have to kick your ass and seeing how we are now friends you can buy my next glass of that piss water they serve in this goddamn whorehouse they have the balls to call a saloon." Seeing that her glass was already empty, I ordered a round for the three of us.

It wasn't long after that that Calamity Jane said there was a bullwhacker down at the other end of the bar and, as she put it, "I need to go down there and rattle his balls." Picking up her half-full glass, she left us with a, "I'll see you assholes later," and then moved on down the bar.

I watched her go then turned to Charlie and all I could say was, "Wow!"

Charlie chuckled and said, "She's quite a woman, isn't she?"

"I'll say," I answered. "I haven't heard many men, let alone any woman, swear like that."

"Hell, that wasn't bad. You should hear her when she gets pissed off at someone."

Charlie being such a refined and distinguished gentleman, I couldn't help but ask how he had met her.

"I hired Calamity and my good friend Wild Bill to be outriders for the supply wagons I brought to Deadwood. I'm not sure that she has done all the things she claims, but I know that she's a dead shot with that rifle she always carries around. Between her and Wild Bill, I felt pretty safe on the trip out here. One of these days, I'll have to introduce you to my friend Wild Bill Hickok."

For a moment, I stood there dumbfounded. "Do you mean the famous lawman that I have read so much about?"

"One and the same, Dell. But don't believe everything you read in those dime novels. He was one hell of lawman and I would guess one of the fastest men, past and present, with a pistol. He is also a very good friend, I'm proud to say but some of these stories in the books have been highly exaggerated and Wild Bill, I'm sad to say, does nothing to dispel them."

"I still would be honored, and look forward to meeting him," I said.

After Calamity Jane had left, Charlie and I finished our drinks and we both decided that it was time to leave. Charlie said he had a meeting with some of the town's fathers to go to and I, with a pretty good buzz on by now, also wanted to leave and locate my two partners.

I bid Charlie goodbye outside the saloon and we went in different directions. I headed in the direction of our campsite. Along the way, I decided that if Indian and Red were not in camp, I would lie down and take an afternoon nap.

The nap was postponed when I reached camp and found Red sitting in the shade smoking his pipe and drinking coffee. Indian was stretched out in another spot of shade sound asleep.

When I walked up to Red he said, with a smile on his face, "Goddamn, is that you, Dell? Hardly recognized you, boy, all cleaned up. Are you planning on going courting this evening?"

Ignoring his comments about my appearance, I poured myself a cup of coffee and I sat down next to Red and rolled a smoke. After I had the smoke going, I told him about my meeting up with Charlie Utter in the bath house and again when I returned to the same saloon where the three of us had been earlier in the day before I went for a bath. "Red, I have to tell you, the damnest thing happened. While we were having a drink together, Charlie introduced me to this lady who worked for him, by the name of Calamity Jane. Red, you won't believe it until you meet her, but she's dressed like a man and I swear to you Red, I never heard more cuss words coming out of a woman's mouth before."

"Sounds like you had a mighty busy day, boy."

"Busy and interesting and I understand that Wild Bill Hickok is in town."

"Then the rumor about him being in town must be true, because I heard the same thing today myself."

"How about you and Indian? Did you have a good day?"

"Not as exciting as yours, but we did meet Mr. Farnum, who bought a round of drinks for us. He wants to be the first mayor of the city of Deadwood and I believe that was the reason he was buying us drinks. However, he did say something that was very interesting."

"What's that?" I asked.

"The city is starting to sell city lots and there are a few left right on the main street of Deadwood and I was thinking we should buy a couple of lots that are located side by side. What do you think, Dell?"

I shrugged my shoulders and said, "Sure, but what the hell are we going to do with the land, or as you call them lots, after we buy them?"

"We hold them for a month or two then resell them at a profit. The way people are coming to Deadwood, I believe we could double our money."

"Sounds okay to me, but what does Indian think about it?"

"Said he didn't give a shit one way or another. Said he would go along with whatever you and I decided."

"Hell, let's go for it," I said. "It would be nice to see what it would feel like to be men of property."

"We are supposed to meet Mr. Farnum at the restaurant for supper tonight and he will have the papers ready for us to sign, if we have decided to buy a couple of lots."

Seeing how we had a few of hours before it would be time to meet up with Mr. Farnum, I found a shady spot and stretched out and took that nap I had promised myself when I had left the saloon.

31

I woke up two hours later when the shade had moved on and the sun was shining on my face. I heard Red and Indian talking as I sat up and reached for a canteen that was close by. After taking a mouthful, I swished it around in my mouth and then spit the water out trying to get rid of the cotton that had seemed to have grown in my mouth while I was taking my a nap. The next time I tilted the canteen, I must have downed about half the water before putting it down.

Feeling better, I walked over to the campfire and poured myself a cup of strong black coffee. Taking the cup in hand, I walked over to where Red and Indian were sitting. Dropping to the ground next to them, I sat with my back to an old downed tree and pulled out my makin's and started to roll a smoke as Indian said, "About time you woke up there, young fellow. We were afraid you were going to sleep on through today and into tomorrow morning."

I finished making my smoke before I said, "I noticed you were doing a pretty good job of sleeping when I came into camp."

"Hell, Dell, I wasn't sleeping. I was just resting my eyes. I heard you come in from a morning of drinking and didn't want to listen to a drunk rambling away at the mouth, so I kept my eyes closed so you would think I was asleep."

"Resting your eyes, my ass, you were sure doing a lot of snoring."

"I added the noise for effect just so you wouldn't bother me."

Red looked a both of us and then threw his two bits worth into the conversation, by saying, "I was looking forward to a nap myself today but between the two of you making so much noise snoring, I couldn't even doze off. In fact, a couple of the city fathers from Deadwood came out to see if everything was okay in camp. I had to stay awake just to keep people that were passing by from shooting the two of you just so they could put the two of you out of your misery."

Indian said, with a very serious look, "Damn Red, it looks as if Dell and I owe you our lives. To show you my appreciation, I'm going to let you buy my supper tonight. I'm sure Dell will find some way to thank you also."

"You bet Indian, I'm going to let Red buy all the drinks tonight."

Red smiled and said, "Damn, it's good to see how we watch out for one another."

We kept up the banter until Red announced that it was time to head on down to the Grand Central Hotel and meet up with Mr. Farnum for supper.

On the way there, I got the feeling that there were more people moving about than when I was roaming around Deadwood early in the day. I wondered if it was due to miners quitting for the day, businesses closing up, or new arrivals. However, as we made our way down the street, it didn't seem as if any of the businesses that lined the street were closing for the evening. By the time we reached the Grand Central Hotel, I had decided that it had to be miners stopping for the day, and by the surprised and confused looks on many of the faces, I figured they had to be new arrivals to Deadwood. That thought made me smile to myself. I had only been town for a full day and here I was thinking of the new arrivals as latecomers.

When we entered the Grand Central Hotel, we found there was standing room only with people waiting to get seated for supper. The three of us were about to turn around and leave when we heard someone call out Red's name.

Looking around I could see a man that I had never seen before, waving for us to come on over. As we headed over to the table, Red told me that the man that had been waving at us over was Mr. Farnum but that the other two men were strangers.

As soon as we got to the table Mr. Farnum said, "Red, I'm glad you and Indian could make it."

"Happy to be here Mr. Farnum. I would like you to meet my other partner, Dell."

After the handshakes were completed, Mr. Farnum introduced us to the other men at the table. "Gentleman, I would like you to meet a couple of Deadwood's leading citizens, Mr. Seth Bullock and Mr. Sol Star, owners of the best hardware store here in Deadwood."

The three men at the table were well-dressed and clean shaven except for well-maintained mustaches, which was the style of the time. After we had all shaken hands, coffee had been served, and our orders placed, Mr. Farnum said, "Red, I hope you don't mind that I invited Mr. Bullock and Mr. Star to dinner. We are kind of having a small celebration. I was elected Mayor of Deadwood this afternoon and Mr. Star has been elected councilman. Mr. Bullock has a lot of experience as a lawman and we hope to get a badge on him soon."

Red spoke for the three of us as he said, "We didn't mind at all and are glad to meet Mr. Bullock and Mr. Star." After a moment's hesitation, Red added, "Seems

I've heard of a lawman named Seth Bullock working in the Montana area."

Mr. Bullock nodded his head and looked Red over trying to see if he could place him, and at the same time said, "I'm from that area but can't recall if we have met before, sir."

"Nope, I never had the honor, Mr. Bullock, but I did scout for the army in Montana and heard the name a few times. If you are one and the same, Deadwood will be a better place by having you here."

It wasn't long after that that the food arrived at our table and we all went to work on that. During our meal the talk around the table had a lot to do with what was happening in and around Deadwood and of course the fact that Wild Bill Hickok was in town.

After the dishes were removed, we all pushed our chairs back and lit up our smokes and sipped coffee.

Mr. Star said, "Being a bachelor and a damn poor cook, that was a mighty fine meal."

We must have all agreed that the meal had been excellent because all of us had cleared our plates. On this trip to the Grand Central Hotel, we didn't get to see Aunt Lou and tell her that she had served up another fine meal. That was probably due to the fact that the place was very busy and the kitchen required her full attention.

While we were relaxing, Mr. Farnum was the first to bring up the subject as to why we were gathering together in the first place.

"Well, Red, have you and the boys talked it over about buying a couple of city lots? The reason we are pushing the sale of lots is the fact that the city could use the money to make some badly needed improvements here in Deadwood. Also we want to legalize and register the city lots so that there are no misunderstandings later."

Red answered for all of us, "We decided on taking two lots, Mr. Farnum."

"Very good," Mr. Farnum said. "I took the liberty of having the paperwork written up and all it will require is for the three of you to sign it."

Mr. Farnum handed the paperwork to Red who handed the paperwork to me. I read it through and it seemed in order to me. The last page showed the layout of the town and the location of our two lots on the main street of Deadwood. I was surprised at the cost of two small lots but then I had nothing to base my notion on. After reading it through, I nodded to Red and then handed the paperwork to Indian who read it through. I noted the surprised look on Mr. Farnum's face as he watched Indian read the paperwork. I'm sure no one at the table, other than Red and I, figured they would ever see an Indian who could read let alone understand a legal document. They were even more surprised when Indian said, "I don't see anything in the paperwork about the corners of the lots having been staked out" as he handed the paperwork back to Red.

Red held the paperwork for a moment then said, "I think we have a deal pending the four corners of each lot be staked out and their location noted on the paperwork."

Mr. Farnum nodded his head and said, "That can be done. If you will stop by Mr. Bullock's and Mr. Star's hardware store around noon tomorrow, I'll have all the paperwork ready and we can finalize the deal. We are working out of the hardware store because they have the best safe in town to hold the town's money."

Red looked over at Mr. Star and asked, "Mr. Star, seeing how you have the best safe in Deadwood, what are the chances of us storing our gold in your safe. I for one am getting sick of carrying these damn saddle bags, everyplace I go. We would be more than happy to pay for that service."

"I would be happy to help you gentlemen out. When we leave here, I'll be heading back to the store to do some paperwork and if you will accompany me, we'll lock up your saddle bags tonight."

It wasn't long after that that we left the restaurant. We shook hands with Farnum and Bullock as they departed and the three of us went with Star to the hardware store. We watched Mr. Star lock up our saddlebags and then thanked him for his help and soon after Red, Indian and I left the store.

32

Once the three of us were back on the street and under a bright moon and stars, we decided that it was time for an after-dinner drink. Besides, we had taken afternoon naps so we weren't tired enough to be crawling into our bedrolls this early.

The first saloon we came to was called the No. 10 saloon. Why it was named No. 10, I have no idea. The inside was lit by several lanterns placed around the interior of the saloon but that still left the saloon on the dark side. Coming into the saloon after being out in the bright moonlight night, the saloon was full of dark moving shadows and it took us a minute or two to get our eyes adjusted to the condition.

All the tables in the saloon seemed to be filled with men playing cards or just sitting around doing some serious drinking. We spotted a place at the bar where the three of us could belly up and order a round.

After our drinks arrived, Indian and I rolled smokes and Red fired up his pipe. Once I had my smoke going, I scanned the room noting that there were several prostitutes making the rounds of the tables looking for drinks or customers. I also spotted our young friend Billy sitting at a table with four other young men and whatever Billy was telling them he had their full attention.

I returned my attention to my two friends and it wasn't long after that someone at my side, "Hello, Dell."

Turning, I saw that Charlie Utter was standing at my side.

I was happy to see him because I wanted to introduce him to Red and Indian. He was a man that you just couldn't help but like. After the introductions were made, I was happy to see that there had been no hesitation or surprise on his part when he met my friends. I had the feeling that Charlie Utter was one of those rare individuals who seemed to like and accept people regardless of color, age, or status in life.

After the introductions and some small talk, Charlie said, "Dell, how would you and your friends, like to come over and sit at my table? I would like to fulfill my promise to you about meeting my friend Wild Bill Hickok."

"Goddamn Charlie, I would consider it a great honor."

Charlie turned to Red and Indian and asked, "How about you, boys? It's just Hickok and me at the table so there is plenty of room."

Red and Indian nodded and Red said, "I would much prefer to be sitting at a table than stand here at the bar being elbowed around."

As we made our way to Charlie's table, I had my first look at Mr. Hickok. I would have placed his age about the same as Charlie Utter's. My guess would be in his middle forties. He wore his hair long and well-groomed the same as Charlie did and had a mustache that covered his upper lip and extended down alongside of his mouth almost to chin level. It was the style of the time and you could probably find a couple of hundred men in Deadwood with the same style mustache. He was wearing a buckskin jacket and was sitting with his back to the wall sipping on a whiskey.

As soon as Mr. Hickok learned that Red and Indian were former army scouts, they hit it off. Although the three of them had never crossed paths before they soon discovered that they knew many of the same people.

Charlie Utter and I sat there enjoying the conversation that passed between the three of them until Hickok said, "Do any of you fellows know that young man in the red checkered shirt that is sitting three tables down from us?"

Red and Indian glanced over to the table Hickok had mentioned. I had my back to the table he had indicated but I didn't turn to look because I knew he was referring to Billy. I had had the feeling that Billy was staring holes in my back ever since we had walked past his table on our way to Hickok's table.

Red said, "Yeah, we know him. He rode into Deadwood with us after we found him wandering around in the woods. He said his entire party was wiped out by the Sioux."

"Then it's true that he had a four- or five-day gun battle with a large group of Sioux?" Charlie Utter asked with a surprised look on his face.

The three of us started to laugh and I asked, "What gun battle are you talking about?"

Charlie said, "Well, according to what the young fellow is telling everyone, he and his crew were attacked in the early hours of the morning by a large band of Indians who made off with their horses. They made their stand in some downed trees and the fight lasted for four days. Said all members of his party were picked off one at a time until he was the only one left. After all his friends were killed, he said, he made his escape, under the cover of darkness, and finally made his way to Deadwood on foot."

Red laughed and said, "No shit! Is that what he is saying?"

"That sure is different than the story he told us when

we picked him up," I said and then went on to relate the story that Billy had told us. "He told us that he had been out scouting the area and hunting game when his party was attacked. He said he heard the shooting but by the time he got back to his friends, he was too late to help. While staying hidden, he was able to see that all of his party had been wiped out. Knowing that there was nothing he could do, he made his escape. A couple of days later we met up with him and he rode in to Deadwood with us," I said.

Indian added, "He sure as hell is no woodsman. We heard him coming through the woods a good ten minutes before we were able to see him. He made so much noise that an Indian could have followed blindfolded. I back-tracked him for several miles to see if he was being followed but found nothing."

"Another strange thing about his story," Red said, "was the fact that he was only carrying a sidearm. Hell, you would think if he was out scouting around and hunting game at the same time, he would have taken a horse and a rifle."

Hickok took a sip of whiskey and said, "That sure doesn't make the story he's telling ring true. Shit, if I was going to make a run from a band of Indians, I sure as hell would have taken a rifle and a extra pistol from one of my fallen comrades. The way he keeps looking over this way I get a strong feeling that he doesn't like someone from this table."

"You are probably right Mr. Hickok," I said, "and I'm sure I'm the one that he dislikes. When we picked him up, he wanted to ride double with me. Our horses had been traveling a lot so I wanted to keep my horse as fresh as possible in case we had to make a run for it. I told him he could ride our mule but I think he felt riding a mule was beneath him."

"Nothing wrong with riding a mule. It was my mode of travel when I was a kid. Hell, under some conditions they are better than a horse," Charlie said.

Hickok looked over at me and said, "Dell, if I were you, I wouldn't trust him when my back was turned."

"I hope you are wrong, Mr. Hickok, I don't want any trouble with him. Besides, he will probably get over his mad after a few days."

"I hope you are right, Dell," Hickok said. "But I don't think that will happen."

A short time later Hickok said that a chair at one of the poker tables was opening up and he excused himself and left to join the game. We shook hands with Hickok as he stood to leave. I didn't know it at the time but that would be the last time I was to see him.

It wasn't long after that that our party broke up. Charlie Utter went his way and Red, Indian, and I headed back in the direction of our camp. Along the way we passed a tent, with an open front, with a sign that said fresh vegetables for sale. A closer look at the vegetables would tell you that they weren't all that fresh but would do for what I wanted.

I told Red and Indian that I would see them back at camp in about an hour. "I want to look in on Old Pain-in-the-Ass."

I went into the vegetable tent and bought a large bundle of wilted looking carrots. After paying the owner an outrageous price for the carrots, I headed for the stable.

The stable man wasn't around but Old Pain-in-the-Ass wasn't inside the barn. I found him out back in the corral working on some hay.

I walked up to the corral and stood there with the carrots behind my back and said, "Hello, Pain-in-the-Ass."

The mule raised his head and glanced at me and lowered his head as if I was someone to be ignored.

I asked, "You're not pissed about being corralled up, are you?"

When he continued to ignore me, I took the carrots from behind my back and waved them in front of me and said, "Look at what old Dell, the man that carries the same nickname as you, has brought you."

This time Old Pain-in-the-Ass looked up with a little more interest. He finally decided that it might be in his interest to come over and see what I had. As he came close to me, he picked up the scent of the carrots and then picked up the pace.

By the time Old Pain-in-the-Ass had eaten all the carrots, he had forgiven me and we were old comrades once again.

33

The next morning, we slid out of our bedrolls while the sky was still gray and had breakfast at the Grand Central Hotel. We thought we might find the restaurant closed at that early hour but to our surprise it was open with most of the tables full of people eating.

While we were working on our coffee and waiting for our food to arrive, we started a list of supplies we were going to need when we rode out to our claim. As I wrote, Red and Indian called out the items and amount that we would need.

After our food had arrived, our table was quiet while we ate. I guess we all knew that there wouldn't be much more restaurant food for us once we headed back to our claim.

When the plates were taken away, we sat back and enjoyed our smokes while sipping on coffee. We also added a few more items to our list that we had thought of while eating.

We left the Grand Central Hotel and wandered around the main street of Deadwood. When we came to the Chinese part of Deadwood, I remembered the dirty clothes that I had left to be cleaned. Searching my pockets, I found the piece of paper that had the Chinese writing on it and we headed for the shop.

Once again, I could smell the food that was being cooked by the vendors in front of their shops and again I promised myself that one of these days I was going to have to come back to Chinatown and try some of those wonderful-smelling Chinese dishes.

When we entered the door, the same old man greeted us that had waited on me when I had left my clothes the first time I was in the shop.

"Welcome to my humble shop," the old man greeted us and then bowed. It didn't take him long to have me bowing to him also.

I laid the piece of paper with the Chinese writing on it on the counter but the old man didn't even look at it when he said, "One moment please." Bowing again he left the room to only return a moment later with my clothes cleaned, pressed, and folded.

After he told me the cost, I was very surprised at the low price. I wasn't sure if I was supposed to give him a tip but in the end, I gave him what he had asked for and then bowed and said, "Thank you."

"You come again soon, yes?"

"Yes," I responded.

Once again he hurried around the counter and opened the door for us, bowing as we each passed by him on our way out.

Out in the street Red turned to Indian and said, "Dell sure does have that bowing down perty damn good doesn't he, Indian?"

"He does indeed," Indian said and then added his thoughts. "You think he might have a little bit of Chinese blood in him?"

Red scratched his several-day-old whiskers as if in deep thought and then said, "Now that you bring it up, he does have those narrow eyes that are common to the Chinese people. I didn't think much about it before. I always figured it was due to him squinting into the sun too frequently but now that you have brought it up you have given me something to think on."

Indian looked over at me as if he was taking a hard look at me for the first time and started nodding his head as he said, "Damned if you're not right, Red. God, you really don't get to know a man until you have ridden with him for a while, do you?"

I continued to walk down the street in silence as if they had gotten under my skin so that they could enjoy their banter all the more. I was enjoying it as much as they were, but didn't let it show. I knew that if I said anything it would only be like adding fuel to a fire.

We continued down the street until we came to a general store and turned in. From the supplies that were on the shelves, we figured we might get everything that we needed in one location. The prices noted on the goods were on the steep side. But then, the items had been shipped in through some rough country so I reckon it wouldn't be any better or cheaper in any of the other general stores in Deadwood.

I removed the list that we had made while having our breakfast at the restaurant from my pocket and handed it over to the man behind the counter and asked if he could fill it for us.

The gentleman took the list from me and looked it over. After a few moments, he looked up and said, "I believe I have about everything on our list except I'm not sure if I have the amount of ammunition you're requesting. You're not planning to start a war, are you?" The owner laughed aloud at his own joke. When he looked up, with a smile on his face, and saw that we weren't laughing at his joke, he lost the smile in a hurry.

Putting his business face back in place he said, "I'll do the best I can. However, I have a couple of other orders to fill first. If you'll return in about an hour or two, I should have it ready."

"That will be fine," Red answered. "We will see you then and thank you."

We left the general store and went back onto the street. Red said, "I think it's about time to head on over to Bullock and Star's hardware store and sign those papers and pick up our saddlebags."

When we entered the store Bullock was waiting on a customer and Star was at a desk that was located in a far corner of the store doing some paperwork. Bullock nodded and at us and said, "Star has the paper work ready for you. You can head on back and he'll take care of you."

As we passed by Bullock, he said, "Dell, could I see you for a moment?"

"Sure, Mr. Bullock," I answered and when I stopped, he excused himself from his customer for a moment and walked with me to about midway in the store. He said, "Dell, I seen Mr. Utter late last night and he said he was afraid he might miss you before you left town. He knew you were going to be stopping by the store this morning so he asked if I would pass along a note when I saw you." With that, Mr. Bullock handed me a folded piece of paper. I thanked him as he turned away and went back to his customers at the front of the store.

I stood where I was and opened the note and read the contents, then refolded the piece of paper and placed it into my shirt pocket.

When I rejoined Red and Indian, Mr. Star was handing the property deeds to Red who in turn handed the paperwork to Indian.

Indian looked the paper over and when he was satisfied that the changes that he had requested had been made, he returned the paperwork to Red and nodded his head.

Our gold was removed from the safe and the amount of gold required to pay for the two lots was weighed out and then Red, Indian, and I put our names on the deed. As simple as that, Red, Indian, and I became landowners in Deadwood. Taking the remaining gold, which I might say was a bit lighter than when we had arrived in Deadwood, with us, we left the hardware store.

The three of us decided to walk down to our two lots to have a look-see. With the paper that was the deed of ownership, a map of Deadwood was attached showing the exact location of our lots and where the corner stakes for both lots where located.

It didn't take us long to find our two lots. I was surprised to see that on both sides of our lots men were putting up tents. We stood at the center line of our two lots for a moment and then Red shrugged his shoulders, and said, "As long as we are close to our campsite, let's get our horses, pack our gear, and then go have a talk with the stable man about spending the night in the livery stable."

At the time I didn't know why Red wanted to spend the night in the livery stable but I would follow his orders to hell and back if he said that was the way we were going.

Later, I learned that Red and Indian had talked about our departure date, while I was running around Deadwood. They had decided that by spending the last day in Deadwood in the livery stable they could pretty well pick any time of the day or night to head out of Deadwood. Considering the amount of gold and supplies we were carrying and the many unsavory characters in Deadwood this would work to our advantage.

Next, we returned to the general store to pick up our supplies. The store owner said he was able to fill our order completely which included all the ammunition we had ordered. We paid the owner in gold and picked up our supplies and headed for the livery stable.

At the livery stable, Red told the stable man that we planned to leave Deadwood after sunrise the next day and that we would like to spend the night at the stable. The stable man hesitated and then said, “I live over at the hotel and I like to sleep in until breakfast, which comes free with the room rent.”

“That shouldn’t be a problem,” Red said. “We would pay our stable fee now, including tonight’s stay. Hell, we would be happy to throw in an additional five dollars for you for helping us out.”

I sweetened the pot by telling him, “We could take care of your customers for the rest of the day and you could take the rest of the day off.”

Indian tipped the scale by saying, “Of course, we will be paying in gold.”

It was too much for the livery stable man and he said, “Goddamn. You know I haven’t had a day off in weeks. You boys have yourselves a deal.”

As soon as we had paid our bill, the stable man couldn’t wait to get out of there. We stood at the stable door and watched him make a beeline for the nearest saloon which, I might add, wasn’t far off.

Red said, “It won’t be long before it’s all over Deadwood that we bought property and supplies, and paid our stable bill in gold.”

Nodding his head, Indian smiled and said, “And they will also know, we will be leaving after sunrise tomorrow morning.”

Not wanting to be left out of the conversation all I could come up with was, “That’s for damn sure.”

“Let’s let the rumor spread for about an hour and

then we will pack up and get the hell out of Deadwood," Red said.

We spent the next hour hanging around the stable's front door, smoking and talking when Red finally said, "Well, Dell, are you going to share with us or are you planning to keep it to yourself?"

Indian added, "Hell, Red, seeing how Dell has all those new friends maybe he is planning to split up our threesome."

"Is that how you're going to treat your two oldest friends, Dell?" Red asked.

Looking from one to the other, I asked, "What the hell are you two talking about?"

As soon as they got a rise out of me, I could see the smile starting to form at the corners of their mouths, I added, "I don't see why in the hell I put up with a couple of goddamn old farts like the two of you."

"You don't think for a moment that a couple of sharp old trail hands like Indian and me would miss seeing Bullock handing you a note."

"Damn. I forgot about the note," I said as I made a big show of searching my pockets looking for the note and making sure that the last place I checked was the shirt pocket where I had put it. Taking the note out. I read it to myself one more time and said, "Hmmmmm," as I folded it and started to place it back into my shirt pocket.

"Looks to me like we are just going to have to beat the information out of him, Indian."

"Sure looks that way, Red," Indian said, as both men took a step in my direction.

"Hold on there a moment, guys. You want to know what the note said? Shit, if that's the problem, I'd be more then happy to read it aloud." As I took the note back out of my pocket, I added, to no one in particular, "A man just can't have any privacy around the two of you."

Holding the note in my hand, I read it aloud. " 'Dell, I'm leaving this note with Mr. Bullock as I know you have some business with him and Star in the morning. I'll be leaving town early tomorrow and may not have the chance to see you before I head out. My friend Hickok asked me to pass the following information on to you. Last night while he was playing poker, he overheard Billy (the kid that road into Deadwood with you) boasting at the next table over from him. Billy was telling some men about his big fight with Sioux Indians. It seems one of the men at the table said that he had heard that he had rode into Deadwood on a mule with three other prospectors. Billy claimed that was a goddamn lie being spread around Deadwood by you and if you didn't learn to keep your mouth shut, he was going to call you out as the liar that you are and put a bullet in you. Both Hickok and I don't feel he has the guts to face someone face-to-face in a fair fight. Hickok said he has the look of a back-shooter so use care. The note is signed 'Your friend, Charlie Utter.' "

After minute or two of silence, Red said, "I have to agree with Hickok. I don't like or trust that little son-of-a-bitch. I'm for looking him up right now and shooting the little shit so we won't have to worry about him."

"Hell, Red, we will be leaving town soon and then he will have to find someone else to blame in his feeble little brain," I said.

"I hope you are right, Dell, or you may have to end up killing him anyway," added Indian.

The thought of killing yet another man gave me a sour stomach.

We had allotted the stable man time to spread the rumor that we were going to spend the night in the stable and leave at sunrise. We also felt that if anyone was interested in our comings and goings, we had given enough time for them to hear about our plans.

It was shortly after that Red said, "Let's pack up and put some distance between us and Deadwood while we have a few more hours of daylight left."

I went back and led Old Pain-in-the-Ass back into the stable. After I put the packsaddle on, he stood still as we loaded him down with our supplies. I figured Old Pain-in-the-Ass was standing still because he knew that he was finally getting out of the stable jail and back to roaming free at night.

The horses also seemed happy to get saddled up. Seeing that our animals had been traveling for most of the year they were also happy and ready to get back on the trail. Hell, I would be the first to admit that I was happy to be getting back to the back country myself. Deadwood had many wonderful things to see and do but being around so many people had a way of wearing on a man.

We left by the back door of the livery stable and from there we took the shortest route to the tree line. Once in the tree line, we each took up our positions, Indian out front, with Red next, then Old Pain-in-the-Ass and me bringing up the rear.

34

As soon as we were about a mile into the tree line, we started to alter our course. We changed directions many times during the day. Whenever Indian found any terrain that would make it hard for anyone following us, he would lead us through it.

Our animals were fresh so we pushed on through the day, covering a lot of miles. When we had about two hours before sunset, Red called a halt so that we could cook our evening meal before dark. When we had eaten, we still had a little light left so we moved on for a few more miles and then made a cold camp for the night.

Once again, we took turns pulling guard duty during the night. The last one on night guard duty also had the job of gathering dry wood in the morning for our morning fire. By the time the other two got up, there was a fresh hot pot of coffee waiting, which did a lot to start the day off on a positive note.

The mornings were getting chillier each passing day and the chill was lasting longer into the each day.

While we were eating our breakfast and drinking coffee, Old Pain-in-the-Ass wandered into camp from his night of roaming. I think we were all happy to see him in the morning, which meant that we wouldn't have to search the woods looking for him.

For the next several days of travel, the routine didn't change. Indian didn't think we were being followed and if we had been followed at the start we had lost them in the wandering course we took to our claim. However, the mode of travel had been set and it had worked for us in the past, so we saw no reason to change it.

When we finally reached our claim, we checked the surrounding area and found no evidence that anyone had been around. Being back at our claim meant that we could set up a more permanent camp, which allowed us the luxury of staying warmer at night and under cover should it rain.

After we had taken care of the horses and unpacked our gear, we set out our claim markers. We were planning on staying at this spot for some time and this would inform other prospectors that they should stay clear.

For the first few weeks we saw no one in our area and we settled into a daily routine. Two of us worked the claim during the day while the other one looked after the camp and horses and kept guard from attack by hostiles be they white men or Indians.

Each day we would rotate the duties. I was always happy when my turn came for guard duty because the days were starting to grow shorter and the water in the stream seem to get colder at each passing day.

We also started to see more people pass by. Many seemed to be headed for Deadwood but a few were prospectors coming from Deadwood and would stop for coffee and of course try to find out how we were doing gold-wise. They always got the same answer from us. "On a good day we might make wages," was our standard answer.

We had accumulated a fair amount of gold by this time and had decided that it wasn't wise to keep it in camp where passersby might spot it. As Red put it, "With all the gold in camp, it certainly would tempt a dishonest man and it might cause an honest man to lower his standards."

We all agreed that we needed to find a good hiding

place. Some place away from prying eyes but not too far from our camp. Indian was the one who came up with the answer. One day as he was moving the horses to a fresh patch of grass, he noticed an old tree that had a rotted out section at the base of the tree at about ground level. The rotted-out section would be hard to spot for passersby due to brush and tall grass around the base of the tree. We all decided that would be a better location for our gold than having it all in our camp. For added protection, the horses were always staked out in that general area so if anyone was nosing around camp area, the horses would be the first to sound the alarm and warn us. We picked a very dark night and moved most of our gold to that location.

As time passed we started to see more and more people, some just passing by and others prospecting on the river that passed by our claim. Several times prospectors would stake claims on either side of us. Some would stay a week or two and then pull up their markers and move on. The prospectors that stayed the longest were the ones that worked downstream from us. However, we had worked that area earlier and had about panned it out so the latecomers soon moved on.

It was during one of these visits from passersby that we heard Wild Bill Hickok had been shot from behind by some young drunk by the name of Jack McCall. I felt saddened by the news as I had found Hickok to be an honorable man.

What surprised me even more was the fact that after a quick trial they had turned the man loose.

A few years later, I learned that that mistake had been rectified. McCall was arrested in Laramie, Wyoming and stood trial in South Dakota for Hickok's murder. The Dakota court claimed that the trial held in Deadwood had not been legal because Deadwood was located in Indian

Territory and not officially part of the United States; as a result, Deadwood had no legal authority to hold the trial. In the second trial in South Dakota, McCall was found guilty of murder and hanged. I, for one, was happy they had got it right the second time around.

Since the day we had left Deadwood, we hadn't encountered any Indians, which made me happy. We did hear that a group of men had left Deadwood and were on their way to Crook City when they had all been killed by Indians. Other then that, things had been fairly quiet as far as we were aware.

35

The all-quiet abruptly ended early one afternoon, when we heard rifle shots coming from upriver. The shots were close enough to our camp that we felt we should investigate. We quickly saddled up and headed upstream. About a quarter-mile from camp we came upon three men holding up behind some river log that had drifted ashore during some past storm. We stayed in the tree line until we were able to call out and identify ourselves as white men and friendly.

Three men came out of the dead trees to greet us. From the way the three men were talking and walking you could tell that all of them had been drinking heavily. It took a while for them to tell us what had happened. When we finally had it all pieced together, it went something like this.

They had left Deadwood several days ago to do some prospecting but were having no luck. Seeing how they weren't finding any gold they started sampling the large supply of the whiskey they had brought with them.

Just looking at them, you could tell that all three of them were heavy drinkers. It seems they had overdone it with the whiskey and forgot to unsaddle the horses and unpack their gear. They claimed that while their backs were turned three redskins made off with their horses, their pack horse, and all their supplies. They said they got off a few rounds but by that time the Indians were well into the tree line.

At first, they wanted us to loan them our horses so

they could take after the Indians. I had to laugh to myself at the idea of us loaning three drunks the use of our horses.

After a moment Red said, "Let me and my partners talk it over in private for a few minutes and we'll see what we can come up with."

We rode off to the side where they couldn't overhear us talking among ourselves.

Red went first and said, "I think we have a couple of choices. We can say to hell with the damn fools or give them enough food and head them in the direction of Deadwood."

"If we give them enough supplies to get to Deadwood, it sure as hell will cut into our supply," I added.

"Dell, is right, "Indian said, "that would sure limit our stay at the claim."

"Does anyone have an idea?" Red asked no one in particular.

"There might be another way, Red," Indian said.

"What's that?"

"Those boys look like heavy drinkers and my guess is that they had more whiskey in their pack because they sure as hell weren't rationing it. The way I figure it," Indian continued, "the Indians will think they won't be followed on foot so they are going to want to take a look at their spoils and also want to lighten the load of items they have no use for. When they find the whiskey, and I'm sure they will, they are going to start drinking and that is going to slow them down and make them get sloppy about covering their trail. I'm thinking, if we trail after them, we might find them easy pickin's."

Red said, "That sounds good to me and if we have no luck catching up to the Indians, we can then decide how we are going to supply those damn fools with food."

We rode back to where the three men were standing and told them our intentions. I think they would have liked to have argued about them taking our horses but we didn't give them a choice in the matter.

Red said, "You boys hunker down here for the night so we can find you in the morning after we see if we have any luck in getting your horses back."

With that said, the three of us rode back into the tree line and out of sight of the men in their tree fort when Red called a halt and said, "As much as the three of us would all like to go chasing after the redskins, I think it would be wise for one of us to stay in camp to protect our interests in our claim."

When Red said that, my old heart sank. I knew the logical choice for the one to stay behind was me. Both Red and Indian had more experience. Hell, I have to admit, the idea of getting out of camp and breaking up the daily routine had given me something to look forward to. I guess the mining business was starting to bore the shit out of me.

So, I was real surprised when Red said, "Why don't you boys chase after those Indians and I'll hang around the claim. God knows it would be a pleasure not having you two around under foot for a spell."

I was thrilled with the decision. However, Red gave us some advice before we rode off, "Don't you boys take any unnecessary chances. It wouldn't do to get killed over someone else's stupidity and Dell, goddamn it you listen and do whatever Indian tells you."

Indian nodded and I said, "Yes sir."

"Okay then, get the hell out of here."

Indian soon picked up their trail and we moved out smartly with Indian leading the way.

We only traveled about five miles when Indian

stopped, dismounted, and walked to his right about fifteen feet and picked up an empty whiskey bottle. Indian smelled the bottle opening and looked over at me with a smile and said, "They have found the whiskey."

After that, the trail got much easier to follow as the Indians made no further effort in hiding their tracks.

We kept coming to locations were they would stop for a short time and mill around. Indian said that they were probably stopping to pass a bottle around.

Two hours later Indian raised his hand for a halt and cocked his head to one side and listened. I did the same but didn't hear anything. Indian motioned me forward. When I was alongside him, he said in a very quiet voice, "From here on we will go very quiet. Soon we will be leaving the horses and go on foot." I nodded my head and understood and we pulled our rifles from the saddle holsters.

A little further on Indian raised his hand for another halt and listened. This time, after a moment or two, I could make out sounds but they were undistinguishable.

Indian dismounted and I did the same. In a whisper, he said, "From here on we go on foot. Watch me. If I stop, you stop and don't move until I give you an okay sign."

He didn't really have to tell me. Hell, wild Indians scared the living daylights out of me. We kept moving forward. Soon we were on hands and knees and then our bellies worming our way forward.

When Indian stopped again, I could clearly hear the redskins, which Indian told me later were Sioux, talking and laughing. Indian held his position for several minutes before he motioned for me move on up and patted the ground next to him.

Slowly and quietly, I moved forward until I lay beside Indian and peeked through the tall grass in front of me.

We were located in a bushy edge of a small clearing. The Sioux were standing in the clearing, drinking and slapping each other on the shoulder and laughing. Their mounts were tied to a tree on the left side of the clearing along with the prospectors' horses and pack horse with the pack still in place.

We lay there watching them pass a bottle of whiskey back and forth and from their actions you could tell they were all drunker than skunks. They were working on a fresh bottle with two more full ones on the ground over by the horses.

After watching them kill that bottle in about ten minutes and then start on the other, one of the bucks, who looked to be no more then about fourteen, sat down on a rock and was very quiet for about a minute or two before his head started to hang. Then his whole body started to lean forward until his center of gravity was well past his feet and he rolled off the rock onto the ground. The way he fell you knew he had passed out.

His two buddys just laughed at him as they passed the bottle between themselves. They were taking long drinks as if they were trying to outdo one another.

One of the two remaining Indians was standing there laughing and the next moment he was sitting on the ground. He sat there for a second or two and then fell over on his back and lay still. The last one standing looked over at his two friends and then raised the bottle, which was about a third full, to his mouth and took a long pull. When he lowered the bottle, there wasn't but a half inch of whiskey left in the bottom. He held the bottle at his side by the neck. He stood there for a minute and then the bottle slipped from his hand and landed on the ground. He tilted his head down and studied the bottle for a moment and a second later his body started to follow his head. He landed face-down on the grass and didn't move.

Another five minutes passed before Indian said in my ear, "Dell, I'm going down there and see if I can take the horses. If you see any of them start to move around, shoot him and then it's to hell with the prospectors' horses and we get the hell of out of here."

With that, Indian stood up and walked boldly into their camp. Before going for the horses he walked around their camp and checked the prints that he was leaving. When he seemed satisfied, he walked over to the prospectors' horses and along the way picked up the full bottle of whiskey. Within a short time he was leading the three horses and the packhorse out of the clearing. The three Sioux never moved a muscle. I gave Indian time to clear their camp before I made my way back to where we had left our horses and we met back up.

We did very little talking while we split the four extra horses between us and moved out at a good clip. For the next hour-and-a-half we covered a lot of ground before we pulled up to give the horses a breather.

Indian looked over and smiled and said "That went pretty damn smooth didn't it."

"It sure did but I have a couple of questions if I may?"

"Fire away, Dell."

"Why did you leave their horses and weapons?"

"I wanted to give them something to think about. When they wake up and see that the three horses and the pack horse are missing they are going to think they wandered off. Then they are going to find my moccasin foot print. Seeing that their horses and weapons are still there they will start to think that maybe some of their elders passed by and took the horses to teach them a lesson."

"Damn Indian, that's sure as hell taking a lot for granted," I said.

"Sure it is but if you think like an Indian it's not so far-fetched. What do you think a party of Sioux would do if they came upon three white men on their land and all of them were passed out from drinking?"

"Kill them and make short work of it if they were in a hurry," I said.

"You are right and they would expect the same from us."

I still wasn't satisfied so I said, "I have one more question I would like to ask."

"Sure if you make it quick. I'm for moving on just in case I'm dead wrong."

"How come you took time to pick up that bottle of whiskey?"

He looked over at me and gave me his stern Indian look and then said, "No Indian in his right mind could pass up a good bottle of whiskey." He then smiled and said, "I felt it would make a good gift for Red, seeing how he had to stay behind."

It was soon very dark and I was glad I was following Indian. I don't know how he was able to keep going in the dark without losing his sense of direction.

36

It was late at night when we made it back to where the three prospectors were holed up. They were happy to get their horses back but one of the first things they did was check to see if their whiskey was there. When they discovered that it was gone, they looked at Indian and me with suspicion.

I felt I had to say something so I spoke up. "The only reason we were able to catch up with them and get your damn horses back was the fact that they found and drank your whiskey."

"We don't want to give you the wrong impression," one of the prospectors said and then added, "We owe you guys for getting our gear back. I notice you're short one man. I hope he didn't get killed in the process of getting our horses back."

Indian glanced over in the tree line and said, "No, he's fine. He's nearby."

I think Indian felt the same way I did about the three men. As long as you could keep an eye them and have your backs covered, they were all right.

As we were riding out. I heard one of the men say, "Seeing how we are out of whiskey I'm for leaving this damn shit hole and hightailing it back to Deadwood." Another said, "I'm all for that."

When we reached the tree line, I glanced back and saw that all three men had mounted up and then they turned and rode off in the direction of Deadwood. That would be the last we would see of the three.

It was daylight by the time we made it back to our claim and we found Red brewing up a pot of coffee.

You could see the worry lines leave his face as we rode in and as soon as he could see that we were all right, he asked, “Where you able to get them damn fools their horses back?”

“We sure did,” I answered with some pride in my voice.

“Well, you can tell me all about it after you have breakfast.”

That suited me just fine because I was powerful hungry from our all-night ride.

After we had eaten, Indian and I sat there by the fire sipping our coffee as if we had nothing to say about last night. When Red couldn’t take it any longer he said, “Okay you goddamn lowlife polecats, tell me how it went down.”

After another short pause on our part, Red started to give us the old stink-eye look so Indian started to tell our story.

“As you might remember, Red, those prospectors claimed there were only three redskins that made off with their horses. We didn’t have to follow their tracks long before we know we were after a hell of a lot more Indians than three. There must have been at least nine or ten Sioux in that party, wouldn’t you say, Dell?”

“More like about fifteen,” I nodded at Indian. “You know us, Red, we wouldn’t let something as trivial as that bother us.”

“Dell’s right,” Indian said, “we didn’t let their number slow us down for a minute.”

“Those Sioux knew we were after them and they did make a good chase out of it, didn’t they, Indian?”

“They sure did at that. However, we were better

horsemen so we were able to keep within a mile or two of them at all times.

"It was getting about dusk when we noticed that their horses were about played out."

"Yep, it was then that we made our move. Dell rode hard to the right and was able to pass them. You see we wanted to surround them to make sure none were able to get away when we made our move on them."

I said, "When we closed the circle, they knew that they were trapped so they pulled up and dismounted to make their last stand."

"Dell and I had a prearranged signal. When I made this bird call, well, actually it was an eagle call. We warriors make better eagle calls than bird calls. However, when I made the eagle call we both attacked at the same time and from that moment on it was all hand-to-hand combat."

Red looked at us for moment and his shook his head and said, "Let me get this straight. You're trying to tell me that the two of you surrounded fifteen Sioux Indians and then you took them on in hand-to-hand combat?"

"Hell, Red," I said, "under those conditions it's hard to make an accurate head count. Shit, there could have been a few more than fifteen."

Indian nodded his head and said, "Now that I think back on it, there may been eighteen Sioux. Things were getting a little wild about that time as you can understand so I couldn't stop to make an accurate count but there had to be eighteen or more."

I added, "Things sure did get a little wild there for a while but there were enough Sioux to go around."

"I remember one time, while the fight was in full gear, I glanced out of the corner of my eye and I seen that four of them savages had Dell on the ground. I wanted to help him out but at the time I had my hands full. I shouldn't have worried because the next thing I know the four braves that were on Dell went flying through the air in four different directions and old Dell was up and damned if he wasn't helping me out."

I said, "That fight must have gone on for a good hour or more."

"Oh, I'm sure it lasted close to two hours before we had all those Sioux laid out on the ground," Indian said and added, "I tell you Red, it was such a good fight that we left those Indians there to sleep it off. We just gathered up the prospectors' horses and rode out as quickly as possible so we wouldn't disturb the wild Indians any more than we already had."

"Yes," I said as I poured myself another cup of coffee. "That is exactly as it happened."

Red didn't say anything as he rolled a smoke but after he had set fire to the end he said "If you boys don't tell me exactly what happened by the time I get done with my smoke, I'm, going to kick the shit out of both of you."

Indian and I were having a good laugh until we saw that Red's smoke was about half gone before we told him what had actually taken place. When Indian produced the full bottle of whiskey that he hadn't given back to the prospectors, Red's attitude changed in a hurry. When we each had a good slug poured in our coffee Red said, "I have to admit your first story was a hell of lot better than what had really happened."

37

After our incident with the young Sioux Indians, our daily life around our claim returned to a boring routine.

I believe the three of us were becoming very tired of the daily grind of working our claim. The pleasure of finding gold in the bottom of the gold pan was wearing off. Each day we would get started later and later and call it a day earlier. The pain in our backs, from bending over panning for gold, seemed to hurt more with each passing day.

To add to our work, we now had to go to the caved-in bank located on our claim and fill a couple of buckets full of dirt and take it down to the river and then pan out the gold.

All in all, everything was going smoothly and when that happens something was bound to go to hell. That bit of wisdom came to haunt me on a day when I was alone in camp. Indian was out scouting around and at the same time hunting fresh meat. Red had ridden downriver to see some prospectors who were working a claim down that way. Being at our claim had us out of touch of what was happening in Deadwood and the rest of the world. Talking to other prospectors was our only way to keep up to date even if their news was a couple of weeks old.

It was one of those days when I was puttering around came when four prospectors rode in. I knew them all. Three of them had stopped by our camp several times before for coffee and had always been friendly. I also knew the fourth member of their group. He was young Billy, the same young fellow who had rode into Deadwood with us on the back of Old Pain-in-the-Ass, much to his disgust I might add.

I nodded at him and said, "Climb on down, boys. The coffee pot is full and I would be happy to share it with you."

One of the prospectors answered, "That's what I like about you, Dell, you're always friendly with the coffee pot and I know for a fact that I could use a cup of coffee about now."

The others agreed as they dismounted and removed their drinking cups from their packs. I filled their cups and then we all found a spot to squat.

I hadn't said a word to Billy and left that up to him so I was surprised when he said, "Damn, Dell, that is good coffee."

I nodded my head and smiled and said, "Thanks, Billy." He sounded very friendly and I figured he must have gotten over being pissed at me.

After that, we spent a pleasant hour exchanging gossip. They said that Deadwood was fast turning into a fair-sized city and the cost of living there was getting higher each day. It was also mentioned that an agent of George Hearst was in Deadwood buying up claims. The name of Hearst was well known by prospectors. He was the man that had made millions in gold mining in several states. Every time a miner hit paydirt he would hope he would be the next millionaire like Hearst. A few did make it but it was a mighty damn few.

When the prospectors finished off their coffee one of them said, "We had better get moving. I know we will be hitting paydirt around the next corner very soon."

When they mounted up, they thanked me for the coffee and even Billy waved and thanked me. I was glad to see that it seemed he was over his dislike of me.

After they had left, I started to throw a pot of stew together. We were out of meat but I felt sure that Indian would find and bring in a fresh kill. Even if he didn't, I could always go out to the edge of our camp and shoot several squirrels to throw in the pot.

As I puttered around the camp I had to chuckle to myself because when Red got back with the news that he had picked up downstream, I would set there and listen to him and then lay all the up-to-the date news about Deadwood on him. Of course, I would have to tell him if he would just stay in camp and tend to the business at hand instead of traipsing all over the country he too could get all the latest news.

It was while I was adding potatoes to my stew pot, with my back to the woods, that I felt the hair on the neck stand up and I felt that something wasn't right. Straightening up, I listened to the sounds around me trying to figure out what had given me the uneasy feeling when I realized that my uneasiness was due to the lack of sound. Normally you would hear squirrels raising hell in the branches of the trees and birds sounding off. When I started to turn to face the woods and at the same time move my hand to my pistol, I heard the sound of a weapon being cocked and a voice behind me said, "Don't even move and keep your hand well away from your pistol."

I recognized the voice as that of Billy and I said, "Did you come back for another cup of coffee?" I was surprised at how casual my voice sounded when down inside me I was thinking I would soon be dead.

"Turn around real slow, Dell, and keep your hand well away from your pistol. I want you to see it coming when I blow your head off."

I obeyed him to the letter, as I slowly turned to face him. I had several reasons to do as he said. First off, I wanted to see where he was standing. The second was I wanted to stay alive as long as possible. The last reason was that I was hoping Red or Indian would suddenly show up and save my sorry ass.

When I finally got turned around and was facing Billy, he was no more then fifteen feet away and in his hand he had his pistol cocked and pointed right at me.

More than anything right then, I wanted to keep him talking if I could. The longer he talked the better the chances that Red or Indian would show up.

The look on Billy's face told you that he was enjoying himself and he didn't want to pull the trigger too soon and spoil his fun. After I was facing him I could see the smile on his face as he asked, "Are you scared, Dell?"

At the time, I thought what damn fool question that was but I nodded my head and said, "Yes." I wanted to wet my lips and swallow but didn't want to give him the satisfaction of showing my fear.

I asked him a casual voice that even surprised me, "Why the hell are you doing this, Billy?"

"Because I hate your guts and the fact that you are telling lies about me in Deadwood."

"Billy, I haven't been telling lies about you."

For a moment I thought he was going to pull the trigger so I quickly added, "Why don't we sit down and have some coffee and we can talk this over." I could see by the look on his face that this wasn't going to go on much longer but I made one last try and if that failed, I was going to go for my pistol even if I figured I wouldn't make it. "Billy, if you shoot me, Indian and Red are going to hunt you down no matter where you go."

Billy showed the first little bit of fear when I said that. I told myself it's now or never and I was ready to make a move when Old Pain-in-the-Ass took that moment to step out of the woods to Billy's right. The movement must have caught the corner of Billy's eyes because his head and the pistol started to turn automatically in that direction. He only moved a fraction of an inch before he realized his mistake and tried to return the pistol and his attention back on me.

I didn't hesitate; I drew my pistol and fired a fraction of a second before Billy squeezed off a shot. The impact of my bullet threw his arm off and his bullet went wide. My round took him in the chest and he fell over on his back.

I stood where I was for a short time watching him to make sure he didn't raise his gun hand. He lay as he had fallen and I watched his legs twitch a few times and then he was still. Holding my pistol in my hand, ready if needed, I walked over to Billy as I watched his pistol, which he still held in one hand, for any movement. When I reached his side, I could see that he was dead and I holstered my weapon. My shot had taken Billy right dead center in the heart.

I stood by Billy for a moment, swallowed and cleared my throat then said aloud, "Goddamn it, Billy, why did you have to be such a dumb son-of-a-bitch?"

As I was standing there, Red came riding hard into camp with his rifle in his hand.

38

As Red dismounted, he looked me over good and asked, "Are you okay Dell?"

After I nodded that I was okay, he kneeled next to Billy and checked him.

It didn't take him long to come to the same conclusion that I had. "He took one right in the heart. At least he sure as hell didn't suffer."

When he stood up, Red said, "Dell, let's go over to the coffee pot, sit down, and have a cup of coffee. Billy boy here won't mind."

Red poured and handed me a cup and then poured one for himself. We sat down on a large log that had been pulled near the fire for that purpose.

I had killed before but this time it was a whole lot different and it had taken its toll on me. For the first time, I knew the person I killed as an individual. I can't say that I liked Billy, but I never meant him any harm. When I took a sip of my coffee, I noticed that my hand was shaking.

Red was the first to talk. I think he was giving me time to calm down.

"I ran into those prospectors that had stopped by and had coffee with you a little while ago. Of course, I had to chew the fat for a spell. After a bit, they mentioned that one member of their party had turned back and was returning to Deadwood and they said they were glad to see him go. Being the nosey son of a bitch I am, I asked them why. They said that they had taken him along because he claimed to be an Indian fighter. Turned out that he sure wasn't a woodsman and worthless as hell in camp. He expected everything to be done for him. While they were talking about him one of the men mentioned that his name was Billy. Right off I knew who they were talking about and got worried that he might come back to our camp. I made an excuse as to why I had to head back to camp and hightailed it back here. I guess I shouldn't have been worried."

I nodded in Billy's direction and said, "If it hadn't been for Old Pain-in-the-Ass showing up when he did, you would have found me lying over there instead of Billy."

"How did it go down, Dell?"

I went through the whole thing with Red and just as I was finishing up Indian rode in with fresh deer meat.

When he saw Billy on the ground he hesitated for only a moment then rode over and dismounted but didn't ask any questions.

Red said, "Dell, why don't you cut up some meat for the stew pot and Indian and I will take care of our horses while I fill him in on what happened."

I was happy to get some chores to do and I wasn't looking forward to repeating this story over again.

Red and Indian talked for a while and then returned to the coffee pot and waved me over. Red had gotten a bottle of whiskey from our supplies and poured a good-sized shot in all three cups of coffee.

We each took a good swallow and Red said, "Dell, Indian and I have a plan on how we think this should be handled. We think we should find a good spot around here and lay Billy to rest. At first we thought maybe we would take Billy to Deadwood and explain what had happened. The more we thought along those lines, the less we liked it. Deadwood is made up of a bunch of wild and usually drunk prospectors. One minute they could say Billy's death was justified and ten minutes later change their minds and we don't think we need to take that chance."

Indian nodded agreement and added, "Anyway, whatever they would decide would never be legal and we know from what happened to that young fellow that shot Wild Bill Hickok that their actions don't make a hell of a lot of sense. This is Indian Territory, supposedly ruled by the Indians. They don't have a court system and are probably happy if we shoot one another."

Red added, "What we would like to do is that you and I take Billy to a nice spot in the wood and dig a grave. While we do that, Indian will backtrack Billy and find his horse and then take it out several miles, strip it of gear and turn it loose."

Indian added, "We figure Billy had to have gotten the horse in Deadwood and it might find its way back there or be picked up by prospectors or Indians.

"Whatever the case, even if it should eventually make it to Deadwood the trail will be long lost."

Red looked over at me and said, "It's your call, Dell, but Indian and I feel our idea would be the best call."

I thought on it for a minute or two and then nodded to Red and Indian and said, "It sounds good to me. I sure as hell don't like the idea of trusting my faith to bunch of drunken ruffians in Deadwood."

So it was agreed. Indian rode off to find Billy's horse while Red and I loaded Billy across Old Pain-in-the-Ass and took him about a hundred yards away from our camp. As he loaded him, I said aloud to no one in particular, "It all started with Billy having to ride Old Pain-in-the-Ass and because of it he hated me. Because of that hatred, he is now taking his last ride and it's atop Old Pain-in-the-Ass." I fondly rubbed old Pain-in-the-Ass's neck and said to the mule, "He never knew that he was on the back of the best goddamn mule in Indian Territory, or the United States for that matter."

Indian rode back in when we were about to put Billy in the grave and said that his horse and gear had been taken care of.

When we had Billy in the ground and covered, Red and Indian took off their hats and looked over at me.

I took my hat off and closed my eyes and said, "Lord, we lay Billy here to rest. I never did get to know him well and can't remember his last name but then I'm sure you must know him. I'm sorry that I had to kill him but you saw how it went and that he never gave me any choice in the matter. Amen."

After the words, we took Old Pain-in-the-Ass and walked him across the grave several times then raked a few leaves over the site and added a few dried branches and returned to our claim.

39

We worked our claim for a few more weeks but it was getting harder each day. We had to carry the material farther and farther from our digging to the stream to pan out the gold. It didn't help that the nights were getting longer and colder. Each morning it took us longer to warm up and with each passing day the stream continued to get colder.

It was one of those cold mornings when we were all sitting around the morning fire trying to get rid of the overnight chill that seemed to take longer each morning, when Red said, "Boys, with the days getting shorter and colder we need start making plans about what we intend to do when old man winter comes in for good."

Seeing how Red was the one we always looked to about our gold operation, Indian asked what was on both his and my mind. "What do you reckon we should do Red?"

Knowing how Red's mind worked, we knew that he had been giving it some thought before he had brought up the subject so we wanted to hear what he had to say.

Red said, "The way I see it, we have several ways that we could go. We could fort up right here and spend the winter. It would be a mighty cold stay but we would be in place come spring. However, if we want to keep mining our claim next year, we are going to have to invest money into the operation. We will need to build a large sluice box and probably hire a couple of miners to help with the work. Investing money in our claim would be a gamble as the gold could peter out at any time and leave us broke."

Red let Indian and me think that over for a moment or two and then he continued. "We could sell our claim outright and spend the winter in Deadwood and the third option is we could sell out and head back to civilization before winter really sets in."

Red filled his pipe and sat back with a cup of coffee in one hand and let Indian and me ponder on what he had said.

All was quiet for several minutes and I was the first to break the silence. "I'm not all that crazy about the idea of spending the winter here freezing my ass off."

Indian said, "I've been thinking that being a prospector is starting to wear mighty thin."

I asked, "If we were to sell our claim, how would we go about it, Red?"

"I was talking to some prospectors a while back and they said that Mr. George Hearst has an agent in Deadwood who is buying up claims. If we did decide to sell, I think he would be a good contact to start with. If that doesn't pan out, we could try someone else."

I had also heard that Hearst had an agent in Deadwood and it took me a moment to remember where I had heard it. Then I recalled the prospectors had mentioned it on the same day they were in camp with Billy and had coffee with me. Red may have heard it from the same prospectors when he heard that Billy had quit the group. With all the stress from the gunplay and killing of Billy, I had forgotten about it.

After a bit Indian said, "Staying in Deadwood for the winter could get very expensive."

"Also," I added, "if we were to stay in Deadwood for any length of time, we would have to be on guard at all times. Word would surely get around about how much we got for our claim and the two lots we have in town. If we get a fair price, people could start adding up the numbers and it wouldn't take them long to have a fair idea of what we are worth. I'm inclined to believe there are more than a few cutthroats in Deadwood who would be more than happy to try and relieve us of our burden."

Red looked at us for a moment and then said, "If I get the drift right from what you two are saying, your line of thought is that we should sell our claim and our holdings in Deadwood and then head east before the winter sets in." Red paused at this point and looked from Indian to me to see if his assumptions were correct. After both Indian and I nodded our heads yes, Red continued, "I also agree with both of you."

Indian and I sat there for several minutes waiting for Red, who we knew was the boss of our crew, to lay out the plan. Several more minutes passed and he just sat there silently sipping on his coffee and smoking his pipe. I was the one to finally break the silence. I knew damn well that Indian could sit in silence forever and wait Red out, but I sure as hell couldn't, so I said, "Damn it Red, how are we going to go about getting all this done?"

Red broke out in a big-ass smile and with a glance over at Indian, I could see a big-ass grin on his face also and I thought to myself, *Damn it, Dell, you've been set up again.* Without a word between the two of them, they both knew that I couldn't sit there for too long just to wait Red out.

Red, with a smile on his face, said, "The way I figure it, two of us should go to Deadwood and one stay here to guard our claim."

Indian said, "I'll volunteer to stay here and pull guard duty if one of you would bring me back a big apple pie. God knows, I could use some time away from you two. Lately, the only thing that happens around here is Dell asking damn fool questions and Red letting gas regardless of who might be standing behind him. I can write a note saying that I agree to the sale of our lots. That way I won't have to be there to sign the paperwork. Besides, you may need Dell's gun hand when you bring back all that money from the sale of the lots."

"Sounds good to me," Red said, "and while Dell and I are in town, we will drop hints about the three of us staying in Deadwood for the winter."

"Why do that Red, if we're not staying," I asked as I looked over at Indian, remembering what he had just said about my damn-fool questions. He was sitting there looking at me with a smile on his face as if he was saying, "I told you so."

Red was the one that answered my question. "When we leave the goldfields for the last time, we will be hauling a fair amount of gold. Every down-and-outer in Deadwood would like very much to relieve us of that gold. If those people believe we are staying in the area they will have a hard time setting up an ambush along the trail if we leave Deadwood unexpectedly."

"I agree wholeheartedly with Red," Indian added. "In fact, I think the three of us should make a pact here and now that we're not to tell anyone even any of our friends in Deadwood, what we plan to do. It's not that I don't trust them—it's the fact that they may let something slip that could get us killed."

I agreed to the pact and would follow it to the letter but I did feel bad about not being able to tell my friend Charlie Utter goodbye. Then and there, I told myself that I would write him a letter once we were out of the Indian Territory and back in civilization. In fact, the more I thought about it, the better I liked the idea. I had never written a letter in my life and the fact that I might get a letter back from a friend would be a hell of a big deal. I didn't know it at the time but that was to turn out to be a long-term correspondence that would continue well into the later years of our lives.

40

Two days later, after we finished our morning meals, Red and I gathered up what supplies we needed to get to Deadwood. We were going to travel light and make the trip to Deadwood as quickly as possible.

When we had Old Pain-in-the-Ass loaded and were ready to ride out Indian came over and said, "Remember that you don't have me along to depend on, so be careful. I sure don't want to have to spend all of our gold on myself."

"We will be careful," I said, "but we will probably spend whatever we make from the sale of our lots in Deadwood having a good old time."

"Don't spend it all on whiskey and saloon girls. Don't forget to save enough to buy me that apple pie."

"I won't forget your pie. That is, unless some saloon lady makes me an offer I can't refuse."

"I really don't care if you do spend it all on wine and women but you had better not return here if you don't bring me that pie."

Red said, "Well, I guess we are all set Dell," and then he looked over at Indian and added, "You take care, Indian."

Indian waved and said, "You too Red and keep an eye on Pain-in-the-Ass here." As he laughed he was looking at me. I don't think he was referring to the mule.

With that we rode out and before we went fifty feet, the real Old Pain-in-the-Ass moved into place behind Red and that left me to bring up the rear.

We made the trip to Deadwood without incident but I

was amazed at the number of people we met along the way. It seemed that there were prospectors panning for gold on every stream we had to cross on our way to Deadwood. Even if we found a likely place for panning and it was deserted there would be evidence that someone had been there and then moved on. We ran across men digging large holes in the ground, digging in banks, and tunneling in the sides of hills. At a few of the places there were armed guards who let us know that we should keep moving along.

When we finally made it to Deadwood, we came upon it from the same hill as when we had arrived the first time. It gave us an overview as to how much Deadwood had changed. In addition to Main Street there were now several side streets. There was construction going on wherever you looked. From our vantage point you could see people moving around by the hundreds. We sat there for several minutes in amazement. On Main Street boardwalks had been added along the storefronts on both sides of the street. As long as you stayed on Main Street, the boardwalk would keep you out of the mud that made up the street. By the number of horses using the street the mud would be made mostly of animal piss and shit even if it never did rain.

From our vantage point, you could tell that people using the boardwalk were walking mighty slow due to the number of other people trying to use it at the same time.

We made our way down off the hillside and worked our way to the main street of Deadwood. When we passed our two lots they seemed out of place, being empty when every lot around now had a building on it or one being built. We took the horses and Old Pain-in-the-Ass to the livery stable and for once Old Pain-in-the-Ass didn't seem to mind when we locked him up in a stanchion. I think he now knew that we would return for him or maybe he just remembered it was here that he had received the carrots on his last stay.

The proprietor remembered us so there was no need to tell him about Old Pain-in-the-Ass. He looked us over and then asked, with a hopeful look on his face, "Did you get rid of that damn Indian?"

I shook my head no and glanced over my shoulder as if I expected Indian to be there and answered, "He's around here somewhere."

The proprietor made a quick sweep, with his eyes, of all the dark corners in the stable and said, "You tell him, I'll take extra good care of the animals."

"Will do," I answered.

Red and I parted company at the livery stable. We had decided early to split our duties. We didn't want to stay in Deadwood any longer than necessary. While Red went looking for Mr. Hearst's agent, I was to talk to Mr. Farnum, the city mayor, about the sale of our lots. At the same time that we were conducting our business, we would both be dropping hints that we were planning to move to Deadwood and spend the winter in town. Before parting, we decided that we would meet at the Grand Central Hotel at supper time and compare notes.

From the livery stable man, I learned that the mayor had an office in one of the hotels farther on down Main Street. The hotel was pointed out to me by a passerby and I made my way over. I found the mayor at his desk going through some paperwork. When I walked up to the desk, Mr. Farnum recognized me and said, "Dell, how the hell are you? Pull up a chair and sit your ass down."

After we shook hands, I sat down, and he reached into one of his desk drawers and pulled out a bottle of whiskey and two glasses.

While he poured the drinks, he asked about Red and Indian and I explained their whereabouts. As we sipped our whiskey, I also told him our plans about selling our lots.

Mr. Farnum wiped his mustache after taking a drink of his whiskey and said, "That sure as hell won't be a problem. I've had four different parties dropping by the office every few days since you rode out, wanting to buy your lots. The lots in that area are going for about three time as much as you paid. If you would like, I could put out the word to the right people and you can pick the highest bidder. If you stop by in the morning, say about nine, I'll be able to tell you who the highest bidder is and maybe have him here in the office to meet you."

With that done, I asked if Charlie Utter was in town.

"Dell, you missed Charlie by two days. He left and headed east to put together a wagon train with supplies to help Deadwood make it through the coming winter. We expect him back before the snow sets in."

I was sorry that I had missed him and at the same time happy that I wouldn't have to lie to him about staying in Deadwood for the winter.

"Sorry I missed him," I said. "I wanted to tell him how sorry Red, Indian and I were to hear that this friend Wild Bill was killed."

Taking a sip of whiskey, Mr. Farnum nodded and said, "That was a real tragedy and a blow to all of us."

I changed the subject by saying. "We decided to spend the winter in Deadwood instead of out in the cold wilderness. Can you steer me in the direction of someone who rents out dwellings here in town where we can hole up for the winter?"

"Sure can. Here, I'll write down his name and where you are likely to find him."

I took the slip of paper that the mayor had written the information on. I finished up my drink and said, "I had better get out of here and let you get back to work."

Farnum laughed and said, "Had I known in advance the amount of paper work that went with being mayor, I might not have been in such a hurry to take this job. But stop by tomorrow and I should have something on who the highest bidder will be on your lot."

With my main chore completed, I decided to drop by and see the man that had cabins for rent. Following the directions I had received from the mayor, I had no trouble finding the man. I told him I was looking for a place to rent for the winter that could sleep three and be available in a week or so. I hated to lie to the man, so when he said he might have something during that time frame, I paid the first month's rent in advance to help ease my mind.

My next stop was at the Number Ten Saloon where I bought several rounds of drinks for some of the prospectors and people that I had met at one time or another. Each time, I would shift the conversation to the weather saying that the nights were turning mighty chilly back at our claim and, of course, I would drop the hint about Red, Indian, and I moving to Deadwood for the winter.

When I left the saloon, I still had a little time left before I was to meet Red at the restaurant, so I went to the bath house and had a hot bath where I soaked until it was almost time to meet Red.

I got to the restaurant first and walked back to the kitchen to talk to Aunt Lou and asked her if it was possible to buy a whole apple pie.

Aunt Lou chuckled and said, "Sonny, I'm a cook and if I cook it you surely can buy it."

I went on to explain, "One of my partners had to stay in camp when we came to town. He remembers your apple pie and claims it's the best he has ever eaten and let me tell you, he's an expert when it comes to apple pie. He made me promise to bring him back one and I believe if I fail in my mission he might just shoot me."

"Well, bless his heart and I sure would feel bad if he was to shoot you," Aunt Lou said and then added, "Honey, if you are eating here this evening, I'll have one boxed up and ready for you to take with you when you get ready to leave."

With that done, I went back out on the boardwalk and stood with my back to the building wall. I did my part by holding up the building while I waited for Red to show up. The sun felt good and I enjoyed watching the endless line of people pass by. I didn't have too long of a wait before Red showed up.

While we were eating our supper, we brought each other up to date on our activities. I went first and told him what Mr. Farnum had said about our lots and that we were to meet him at nine tomorrow. Red explained that he had talked to George Hearst's agent and was able to convince him to ride out to our claim within the week and if the claim was as Red had said he would make us an offer.

We decided that as long as we had to spend the night in Deadwood we might as well take a room here at the Grand Central Hotel. Before paying our restaurant bill, I made a trip to the kitchen and picked up the apple pie that I had ordered. When I returned to the table Red asked, "What have you got in the box, Dell?"

"That," I answered, "is Indian's apple pie."

"Might get a bit stale by the time you get it to camp."

Chuckling, I said, "I only promised him an apple pie; I didn't promise him how fresh it would be."

We paid our restaurant bill and at the same time

paid for a room for the night. One look at the bed and bedding convinced us to go back to the livery stable and pick up our bedrolls and sleep on the hotel floor.

41

The next morning we were out of our bedrolls long before first light. It sure as hell wasn't what one would call a good night's sleep with all the noise and the occasional gun shots floating up from the streets. One thing was for sure, Deadwood never did sleep.

We rolled our bedrolls and I picked up the box that held Indian's pie and we headed for the restaurant downstairs.

Not a word had passed between Red and me since we had climbed out of our bedrolls this morning. I have traveled with Red too long not to know that he would only bite my head off if I tried to make morning conversation before he had his coffee.

As soon as we were at our table, I ordered a pot of coffee and told the lady that waited on us we would order after we had our coffee.

We sat in silence until the coffee arrived. Red reached for the pot first and poured himself a cup of coffee and picked it up and blew on top of the coffee cup a few minutes and then took his first sip and let out a long sigh. After the second swallow, Red asked, "What time did you say Mr. Farnum would meet us in his office?"

"He said about nine o'clock this morning."

"Hell, a good part of the day will be gone."

"You got that right, but I guess that's the life of a businessman in the city."

"After we have finished eating," Red said, "we could

head on over to the general store and buy a few supplies and leave them in the livery stable with our other gear."

We finished our meal, bought our supplies and stored them with our gear in the livery stable and still had time to kill before our meeting with Mr. Farnum. We stood, with me still holding the boxed pie, leaning against the stable wall having a smoke watching the people go by until we got tired of that. Red butted out his smoke and asked, "Do you reckon there's a saloon close by the mayor's office where we could get a beer while we wait?"

"In this town I would be willing to bet that there is a saloon on one or both sides of the mayor's office."

"Hell, Dell, let's me, you, and your pie go have a beer while we wait."

I was right, there were saloons on both sides of the mayor's office and they were going full blast. Our one beer turned into two before nine o'clock finally rolled around and we headed for the mayor's office.

True to his word, Mr. Farnum had a man in his office who wanted to buy both our lots. After a few minutes of small talk the man looked at his pocket watch and said he had another meeting in half an hour and we got right to the point of our meeting.

He said that he very interested in buying our lots and wanting to build a theater on the two lots. His offer was over three times what we had paid and was slightly over the range Mr. Farnum had quoted to me the day before and I had already passed that information on to Red. Red looked over at me and I nodded my head and then Red turned to man who wanted to build a theater and said, "Looks like we have a deal, sir."

It only took Mr. Farnum a few minutes to draw up the paperwork to transfer the lots from us to the new owner. Indian's letter, which stated that we had the right to sell his interest in the lots, was attached to the new deed.

As soon as the paperwork was signed the new owner paid us in gold coins. Both parties paid recently levied business fees and shortly after that the new owner left.

Red and I stayed a few minutes longer to thank Farnum for his help in closing the deal for us. We offered to take him next door to the saloon and buy him a round of drinks but he declined the offer, saying, "If I went next door for a drink, I would have a hell of time getting back out." And he went on to explain, "Since becoming mayor, it seems like everyone I meet in saloons or on the street has one or two things that they figure need doing or fixing here in Deadwood."

Red said, "I feel for you, Mr. Farnum, but I'm happy it's you and not me. With my poor disposition, I would probably shoot a half-dozen people."

"I have to admit it's not as bad as it used to be. Now that we have business fees coming in we are able to make a few improvements around here for the better."

We left Mr. Farnum shortly after that and headed for the livery stable. In short order we were packed up and we rode out of Deadwood for what was to be the last time.

42

We made good time getting back to camp. With so many prospectors coming and going in the area there were now well-worn trails going in and out of Deadwood. You could find a trial in any direction that you might happen to choose.

Indian was in camp to meet us when we rode in. There wasn't time to bring him up to date because the first words out of his mouth were, "Well, did you bring my apple pie?"

When I handed him the box, I said, "I sure as hell am happy to get rid of this box. I had to stand guard over it every night just to keep Red and Old Pain-in-the-Ass from getting into it."

"Besides that," Red said, "we have had Indians and white men on our trail all the way. That damn pie smelled so good we couldn't shake them off our backtrail."

Indian just grunted and took the box and a spoon over to a log at the edge of camp and went to work on the pie. If the pie was stale it sure didn't seem to bother Indian because he didn't stop until the pie was gone and I might add he never offered Red or me a piece.

After Indian finished off the pie, he walked over to where Red and I were sitting next to the fire drinking coffee. As he poured himself a cup of coffee Indian said, to no one in particular, "Damn that was one mighty fine pie."

Red said, "It must have been, seeing how you didn't offer us a piece."

Indian looked from one of us to the other and said, "I

figured that you two had eaten all the pie that you wanted in Deadwood. If you two were so dumb that you didn't have any of Aunt Lou's pie while you were there, I sure as hell don't feel sorry for you."

Both Red and I agreed that we had eaten several pieces of her pie while in Deadwood. We sure as hell didn't want Indian thinking we were that dumb.

Slowly the conversation got around to how we made out while in Deadwood. I brought Indian up to date on the sale of our lots and Red told him about his meeting with George Hearst's mining agents and that the agent had agreed to ride out and take a look at our claim and if he was interested he would make us a offer.

True to his word, the agent rode into camp four days later along with three men. After the introductions were completed, Red took the agent to where we had been working the riverbank. He also explained how we had had good luck panning the stream downriver from our claim and how we had worked our way upriver to this location. Samples that were taken upriver from our claim had not proven out so we figured the gold we found in the river had come from this location.

The agent nodded and said, "The conditions look good but I would like to have my men take some sample digs and see how that pans out."

When Red gave him the okay, the agent set his men to work taking samples at various locations and then panned out the results.

For the rest of the day Red, Indian, and I sat in the shade and watched the four men dig and pan our claim.

As I sat there I wondered aloud, "Between the four of them they are panning up a fair amount of gold."

"That they are," Indian added.

"Who do you reckon that gold belongs to?" I asked.

After a moment Red said, “The way I see it, that gold belongs to us if he doesn’t buy the claim and to him if he buys us out.”

“Sounds fair to me,” I said. “Do we have to pay them a day’s wages for doing all that work if the agent doesn’t buy our claims?”

Indian said, “Hell no. We sure didn’t hire them to work our claim.”

“So, after we take the gold, if he doesn’t buy us out, the agent is responsible for paying the miners?”

Red asked, “Why are you fretting over that Dell?”

I nodded to where the man were working and said, “That pan they are using to store their find in is getting mighty full. If I was to pan that much gold and then see it given to three strangers like us, I would be pissed. I was just trying to get things straight in my mind where we stand if things get out of hand.”

Red said, “Dell, you worry too much.”

Maybe I did but I noticed that Red moved his rifle a little closer and after about ten minutes Indian picked up his rifle and wandered over to the tree line where he sat down in the shade with his back to a big tree with his hat pulled down and his rifle across this legs. Yeah, I guess I worry too much.

However, my worrying was for naught. The agent came over and sat down beside Red and asked, “Would you mind if I help myself to a cup of your coffee?”

“Sure, help yourself,” Red answered.

After the agent had his coffee poured and had taken a few drinks he said, “Red, I believe your claim is everything you said it was. As you have probably already figured out, you are at point where you will need to invest some money in equipment to continue working your claim. The way I see it, a steam engine will be required to run a high-power water hose to cut down the bank where you have been digging."

After taking a few more swallows from his cup to let this information settle in on us, he continued, "A large sluice box will have to be built to handle all the material washed out by the water hose. If one was to start from scratch to get that all done by spring, we are talking about a good deal of money, but it could be done."

Again he waited to see if we had anything we wished to add. We had already come to that conclusion long before we had even spoken to him, so we sat there and waited for him to continue.

When the agent was satisfied that we had nothing to add, he continued, "Here is where I have an advantage over you, boys. The man I'm working for, Mr. Hearst, already has all that equipment left from his mining operations in Montana and some of that is being shipped overland to Deadwood as we speak."

"Your mine would be a big gamble if this equipment wasn't available to me. You can never be one-hundred-percent sure that the gold won't peter out before you can reclaim your initial investment. With the availability of the equipment it makes your claim a good gamble to me. I'm willing to make you an offer of one thousand dollars for the claim. That is about double what I've been offering for most claims in the area."

Red said, "If you will give my partners and me a few minutes alone to talk it over, we will be able to give you an answer."

"Sure, take your time; I'll be over with my men taking a few more test samples."

As soon as the agent walked away, Red motioned Indian over to where we were sitting.

While Indian was drinking a cup of coffee, Red explained what the agent had said to us. When he was finished, he said, "Well, boys, what do you think? Do we accept or reject his offer? Why don't you go first, Dell?"

"Well, we have already agreed that we want to sell and his offer sounded fair to me. I'm for accepting so we can get the hell out of Indian Territory before the really cold weather gets here."

Red looked over at Indian and asked, "How do feel about the offer?"

"I go along with what Dell said, but I don't know anything about the gold mining except what you have shown Dell and me, so I'll leave the final decision up to you."

Red nodded and said, "I think we're all on the same page. We all would like to get out of the mining business. I would hate to like hell to continue to mine our claim and risk losing what we have already made."

Red paused for a moment and looked at both Indian and me to see if we wanted to add anything. After a short period of silence, Red said, "Okay then, I'll call Mr. Hearst's agent over and tell him we accept his offer."

From that point on everything went pretty damn fast. The agent had all the paperwork with him that was required to make the transfer of the claim legal. We signed the documents and the agent handed us a draft of the money, against Mr. Hearst's bank in Montana.

To put the final touch on the transaction the agent brought out a bottle of whiskey and we had a round of drinks.

Over the drinks the agent said that he was going to pull out in the morning but would leave two men here to work and guard the claim and that we could ride into Deadwood with him if we had a mind to. I think it was his friendly way of saying that we weren't welcome to stay on.

Red said, "Thanks for the offer but we plan to be on

our way in about an hour from now. We wanted to use the rest of the daylight hours to be on down the trail." Red didn't say we were going to Deadwood but he also didn't indicate that we weren't.

It took less than an hour for us to pack up and, after saying our goodbyes, we left our claim for the last time.

Over the years, I often wondered if the claim ever paid off for Mr. Hearst and company but I never ran across anyone who knew.

43

We followed the now well-worn trail in the direction of Deadwood for about two miles and then turned east off the trail in a very rocky area. It would be hard for anyone who might be tracking us to determine when or if we had left the main trail.

From that point on, Indian would be out front scouting the trail and we would only see him for a few minutes off and on during the day but he would always show up around the time we started to set up our camp for the night.

During the day, while Indian was out scouting, Red would once again take the lead with Old Pain-in-the-Ass and me following along, bringing up the rear. We had all traveled together for so many miles that everyone, including Old Pain-in-the-Ass, knew his position and duties within the group.

In our travels back to civilization, Indian only spotted one small band of Sioux Indians which he figured was a hunting party. Just to be on the safe side we made a wide swing around them.

The surprising thing about our trip through the Indian territory was the number of white men we met on the trail. It seemed that every day we would cross paths with men who were all heading in the direction of Deadwood. Some would stop and want to chat for a few minutes. Their first question they asked was if we had found gold in the area. Each time we were asked we would claim we went bust and were headed back to our home range for a new grubstake and planned to return next spring and try our luck once again.

Most of the travelers didn't stop to talk. A few would wave as they passed by but many were in such a hurry that I wasn't sure that their animals would ever make it to Deadwood without giving out. They were in a mighty big hurry to get to the goldfields and become rich. I'm sure the closest most of them would ever get to gold would be working for pay in someone else's mine or foundry.

We were making good time despite shorter daylight hours and cooler days and nights. We only ran into one really bad day on the whole trip out of the territory, where we had a light cold drizzle and the wind blew the rain in all different directions all day long and late into the night. It gave you a prelude of what was to come.

It was like a weight being taken off our shoulders when Red announced that by his reckoning we had cleared Indian Territory. For the first time in many days we relaxed somewhat. However, we couldn't become too complacent as there were still many dangers. We still could run into Indian raiding parties or white men who would think nothing of robbing and killing to get something that didn't belong to them.

Should anyone decide that we would be easy pickings they would find the pickings a might hard. The three of us had been traveling together a long time and I'm sure we could dish it out as well as anyone.

44

On our second day out of Indian territory, after about two hours on the trail, Indian rode back from scouting ahead and said we should have a talk.

Red said, "Okay, let's hold up here and make a pot of coffee."

While the coffee was brewing, Indian said, "About five miles in the line of our travel there is a small valley with only one entrance with side hills that are fairly steep. In this valley there are about seventy or more head of cattle with three men keeping them bunched together. What is odd about the setup is if you are making a gathering for a drive why bunch them up so near Indian Territory? You would think they would make the gathering location further east where there is less of a danger of Indians raiding, and take off a few more miles of driving time to get to a railhead."

Red rubbed his several-day-old whiskers and then said, "That is a might bit strange at that. Why don't we mosey over that way and hunker down, where they can't spot us, and have a look-see. Indian, do you think you can get us to a spot were we won't be spotted?"

Indian thought about it for a moment and then nodded his head. "If we circle around them to the north and come at them from that direction, we could do it. On that side, along the top of the rim of the valley, there is a good stand of trees. I'm sure we could get there without being seen."

"Then let's go and have us a look-see," Red said.

Indian led the way and about an hour later in a wooded area he called a halt and said in a quiet voice, "We should tie the animals here and go the rest of the way on foot."

Following Indian's lead we made our way through the wooded area. When we reached the edge of the tree line, we got down on our hands and knees and made our way through tall grass up to the valley's rim until we were able to lie on our stomachs and view the small valley below.

Below was a small herd of cattle and we watched as two outriders, riding in opposite directions around the perimeter of the herd, were pushing back any cattle that started to a wander up the side hills that ringed the small valley. A third man was at the campsite directly below us, sitting by a small fire drinking coffee. As we watched, one of the outriders broke off from his duties and rode into their camp. While he was pouring himself a cup of coffee, the other man saddled his horse and became the new outrider.

We must have lain there studying their routine for about twenty minutes when Indian motioned for us to look towards the valley entrance. I glanced over that way and two more riders entering the opening of the valley floor with fifteen more head of cattle.

We lay there for another ten minutes before Red gave the signal that we should leave our observation post and return to our animals. We didn't speak as we slowly made our way back to the horses and mounted up and left the area. When we were a good five miles away, we pulled up and gave the horses a breather.

Red was the first to speak. "That sure as hell was weird."

I nodded and Indian said, "Like I said earlier, that is a very strange location to make a gathering."

I asked, "Did you notice all the differing brands on those cattle?"

"Sure did," said Red, "and I'd be willing to bet, due to where they are holding those cattle, that those are rustled cattle. Looks to me like they are rustling a few cattle at a time from ranchers east of here and then driving them here until they feel they have enough cattle to make a drive to market."

"Seems to me those boys have a pretty sweet deal worked out for themselves," Indian said. "By driving them in the direction of Indian Territory the ranchers would hesitate following the rustled stock too far, thinking that they might run into Indians."

"And that's only if ranchers spotted the tracks of a few cattle missing from their herd before the tracks get too old to follow," I added.

"What should we do?" Indian asked Red.

"I don't see what we can do. There are five men and we have fair amount of gold that we are carrying that needs our protection. I would hate like hell to lose what we have worked for over the last year plus have any of us get killed over something that is none of our business."

I said, "I just don't like the idea that those men rustling something that someone else worked so hard for."

"Nor do I," Red said. "When we hit a town that has a lawman, we can report it to the law."

With that, we continued on our way. We soon found ourselves in open rolling hills. After spending several months in wooded land the open country seemed strange but still comforting. It sure made for easier travel and the miles were adding up a hell of a lot faster.

45

It was late on the same day that we crested a hill and we spotted a ranch about a half a mile off, with smoke coming out of the ranch house chimney.

We sat on our horses for a spell and just looked the place over. Everything looked very peaceful. Off in the distance we could see a small stream flowing through the property. We didn't see any ranch hands and mighty few cattle.

After a short time Red said, "Seeing how cold the nights are getting that barn looks awful inviting. Do you reckon we should ride on down there and see if we could spend the night in the hayloft?"

"And just maybe," Indian added, "we might be able to talk our way into a meal that Dell hasn't cooked."

Normally, I would have bitched about that remark but this time I had to agree. A meal cooked by someone other than me did sound damn good.

Seeing how we were all in agreement we rode on down into the ranch yard. We were a bit surprised when we found no ranch hands around the yard. There were a couple of horses and a few mules in the corral but that was it.

Now that we were up close you could also see small things around the ranch that were in need of repair. Things that should be taken care of on a routine basis by the hands. Items like one of the barn's door hinges was coming loose and one of the top corral poles was broken.

Just little things that weren't noticeable from atop the hill.

When we were about forty feet from the front door of the ranch, Red sang out, "Hello the house," which was the customary greeting when riding up to a ranch house and this was done before you were invited to dismount.

After a moment or two, a man opened the door and stepped out with a shotgun held over his shoulder with his finger inside the trigger guard, and asked, "What can I do for you boys?"

Red said, "We were wondering if we could put up in your barn for the night. The nights are getting colder and that ground seems to be getting harder every night."

"Where you boys hailing from?" the rancher asked.

Red was doing the talking and Indian and I allowed him to carry the load. "We're coming out of the Indian Territory by way of Deadwood."

"I've heard of that new town of Deadwood that was located in the middle of Indian Territory but you're the first I've met who have actually been there. It seems like everyone I know is on their way there and that includes all my hands. I have to say, I wish I was headed there myself. You boys climb down and come on in. The coffee's hot."

We dismounted and tied our horses to the hitching rail in front of the porch and entered the ranch house. You could smell the strong odor of coffee and, due to the chill in the late afternoon, felt the warmth of the room as soon as we walked in.

Over coffee the rancher said his name was Robert Kingsley but said most folks called him Bob. After we introduced ourselves, Bob started firing questions at us.

"So," he said, "there really is a town called Deadwood located in the Indian Territory."

We could see he was interested in the news from the

goldfields so we filled him in on what was happening in and around Deadwood. How a few men had made big strikes while many more went bust. We explained how large Deadwood had grown and that more people were coming every day.

"Is it true that Wild Bill Hickok was shot and killed there?"

"It's true," I answered.

"Did you boys get to meet him?" Bob wanted to know.

I nodded and said, "He was a very nice and friendly man."

When Bob finally stopped asking questions we had an opportunity to ask a few of our own.

"How many hands do you have working with you on your spread, Bob? I don't want to be nosey, but we couldn't help but notice that we hadn't run across anyone when we rode in."

"Hell, ever since Custer said there was gold in Indian Territory, all my hands rode out this summer. The few hands I've been able to hire since then only stay long enough to make a grubstake and then they also haul ass for the goldfields."

"No family?" I asked.

"Nope," Bog said. "Lost my wife a few years back. I was a prospector when I met and married her. We settled down here on the ranch and it was a good life until she passed away. I've never been much of a rancher but did all right until I couldn't keep any hands for any length of time. Hell, I can't blame the hands, if I could get out from under this place, I would go back to being a prospector, which was my first love."

Red asked, "How many head of cattle do you run, Bob?"

"Not many anymore. The Indians pick up a few, I sold

a few trying to pay top wages for hands but all that did was allow the hands to build their grubstakes a little faster."

I think the rancher was starting to get the feeling that Red might be a little interested in buying his ranch because he offered to show Red a map that covered the ranch property.

Over more coffee Red, Indian, and I poured over the maps that the rancher had rolled out on the table. We could see that we had ridden over a good part of his range coming in this afternoon. While Red and Indian asked more questions, I went out and put the horses and Pain-in-the Ass in the barn and threw them down a good supply of hay to work on. I also found a barrel of grain with a can inside the barrel and gave each animal a can full.

When I was through with the animals, I returned to the ranch house to find Bob frying steaks and potatoes on the stove. While he was doing that he was telling Indian and Red about all the cattle rustling going on around the area.

"The rustling has been going on around here for the last three or four years. They never take a large number at a time so you don't notice right off but by the time you do, they are long gone. At first, I thought Indians were taking a few head but after comparing notes with other ranchers in the area, I believe it's being done by white men."

I looked over at Red to see if he was going to mention the collection of cattle we had seen in the valley near Indian Territory. One look at him, I figured he had something on his mind so I didn't bring it up. It didn't take long for me to figure out what Red was thinking when he said, "Bob, it sounds like you would like to head for the gold fields and me and the boys have been thinking about settling down."

I don't recall us talking about buying a ranch and settling down but the idea sounded good to me. The thought of living in a home with winter coming on sounded mighty fine.

Red said "We haven't decided on a particular area yet but if the price for your ranch was within our means, we might be interested."

Bob rubbed his chin and said, "Let me think on it for a couple of hours and I'll see what I come up with."

"Sure, take your time. We won't be pulling out until morning."

Old Red was an old horse trader from way back and he was putting the pressure on Bob without Bob realizing it.

No more was said about selling the ranch and as we got up to head for the barn Bob said, "You boys can stay in the bunkhouse tonight. There is a stove in there and wood for a fire."

Bob didn't have to ask us twice and the three of us headed for the bunkhouse to bed down. While Red started a fire, I went to the barn to get our coffee pot, cups, and coffee from our supplies. I didn't want to wake up without the means to make coffee and have Red waiting for Mr. Kingsley to get up and make a pot of coffee so that Red could turn back into a human being.

We sat around drinking coffee and smoking until we saw Mr. Kingsley turn out the lights in the house and then Red said, "If Kingsley should decide to sell his ranch, are we interested in buying?"

Red looked over at me first and I said, "It would be kind of nice to have a place you could call home. Besides, if we decide later on that it's not to our liking we could always resell and move on."

Red turned to Indian asked, "How about you?"

"Like Dell said, if we decide we don't like it, we can always sell. Besides, we were planning to hold up somewhere for the winter so why not here. I wouldn't mind seeing what it's like living on our own cattle ranch rather than working on someone else's spread.

"I agree with both of you. Besides, living in town all winter doesn't settle all that good with me. From what Kingsley told us there is a town about fifteen to twenty miles from here. If we get cabin fever, we can always head for town for a couple of days. Hell, we could have the better part of two worlds."

"What town is that Red?" I asked.

"Kingsley told me and Indian about it while you were in the barn taking care of the horses. Its called New Hope and is located southeast of here."

After that, we put our heads together and had come up with a maximum price we were willing to pay for the ranch and Red said, "Well, it looks like it's up to Kingsley to make the next move so I'm going to bed."

It wasn't long before we were all in a bunk. It was great to climb into bed, in a warm room, with no rocks under you that you missed when you rolled out your bedroll. And best of all, you knew that you wouldn't have to be waking up in the middle of night to stand guard duty out in the cold.

46

We were up before first light which was very normal for us. I stoked the stove and threw in a couple pieces of wood and moved the half-full coffee pot to the center of the stove to heat.

We were just finishing our second cup of coffee when we noticed the lights come on in the kitchen of the ranch house. We waited about fifteen minutes, to give Kingsley a few minutes to get squared away, and then we made our way to the yard water pump and washed up before we headed for the ranch house.

Bob Kingsley was at the stove cooking steaks, potatoes, and a big platter of eggs. The sight of the eggs made my mouth water.

Bob said, "Set on down boys. There's coffee on the table and the food will be done in short order."

When the food was on the table and we had our plates full, Bob asked, "How long do you boys plan to stick around the area?"

Red answered by saying, "We plan to ride into that town that you said was located southeast of here. What was the name of that town again, Bob?"

"New Hope."

"That's right, we were planning to ride over to New Hope and stay there long enough to replenish our supplies and then we are heading southeast. Hell, as long as we can now afford it we might just as well spend the winter in warmer country."

Knowing Red as well as I did, I knew that he was letting Bob know that we had done okay in the goldfields. I remember him telling me once that sometimes you need to prime the pump to get the water flowing when you're trying to make a deal. I figured that was what he was doing to Bob. If Bob was a prospector, as he claimed, the fact that we had done okay in the goldfields was going to get his juices flowing.

Through the rest of the meal Mr. Kingsley was very quiet and in deep thought, while the three of us carried on a continuous conversation among ourselves.

When the meal was over, Red said, "Well, Bob, the boys and me need to be on our way. We thank you for your hospitality and we would be more than happy to pay you room and board for your hospitality."

"There will be no pay required for your stay. I've enjoyed the company and the news."

We started to get up and I thought to myself that Bob had decided to keep the ranch, much to my sorrow.

I told myself that with luck there would be another time and place down the road to find a permanent home. Then when we were all standing, Bob said, "Please sit down a few more minutes, boys."

We complied with his request and he continued, "I've thought it over all last night and this morning and have decided that I'd like to sell the ranch and go do something I've wanted to do since the wife passed away but the ranch held me back."

Bob took a long breath and slowly let it out and said, "I know the ranch needs some work and with a couple hands I could get the job done but until the goldfields go bust it would be damn near impossible to hire hands. With the three of you working together, you wouldn't have that problem about hiring extra hands. I can only guess at how many head of stock I have left." After a few moments of silence he told us what he wanted for the ranch, lock, stock and barrel, with the exception of riding gear and a supply horse that he was going to need to get to the goldfields.

What surprised me about his asking price was the fact that it was several thousand below what we would have been willing to pay.

Red thought about it for a moment and then said, "I would have to talk it over with my partners before I can give you a yes or no."

Bob asked, "Would you like me to give you boys a moment in private to talk it over?"

"If you don't mind, Indian, Dell, and I will go over to the bunk house and have a little discussion between us and let you know."

As soon as we were in the bunk house Red asked, "What do you two think? Should we go for it?"

I said, "I like the deal."

Indian nodded his head and said, "Let's go for it."

"Okay then, we buy the ranch at his price. I think we should hang around the bunk house for about thirty minutes or so before we get back in and say we will buy. We don't want him to think that we are too anxious to accept. He may get the feeling he priced the ranch too low."

As we sat around the bunk house drinking coffee, we watched Bob come out of the house several times, look over at the bunk house. And then pace up and down the porch a few times before disappearing back inside the house.

When Red felt that we had stayed long enough to make it seem like we had discussed it through, we returned to the house and told Bob he had made himself a deal. By the look on Mr. Kingsley's face, I believe he was relieved that the deal had been accepted.

Red said, "If I may, Bob, I would like to make a couple of suggestions."

"Sure, Red, fire away."

"It sounds like you are planning to go into Indian Territory. I heard you say that you had been a prospector in the past so I figure you know the dangers so I won't harp on that, but, I would suggest that you try and find a couple of good men to go along with you. I also noticed you have four mules out in your corral and if I was going back to Deadwood, I would load them up with supplies for resale once you reach Deadwood. Even before we left, prices on food items were starting to climb. I believe you could turn a good penny on whatever you could carry in."

Bob nodded his head and said, "That's a damn good idea and I know two good men who want to go as soon as they get a grubstake."

"Offer to grubstake them for a percentage of what they hit if they help you get your supplies through."

"Damn Red, you sure you don't want to ride along with me?"

Red laughed and said, "No, thank you, I wasn't much of a miner; too damn hard on my old back."

Now that Bob knew that he was going to go to the goldfields to prospect, he was a man possessed. Within three hours, he had loaded, with our help, everything from the ranch that he wanted and said, "What remains you boys can have to use, give away, or burn as you see fit."

We rode out with Bob for the town of New Hope so that we could have the deed for the ranch transferred into our names by a lawyer that Bob said had an office in town.

As we rode away, he took one last look at the ranch over his shoulder and said, "You boys have bought yourself a good ranch. It would have been a good place to raise kids if the wife hadn't passed away." He then looked at us and said, "Maybe one of you can do what I couldn't do and raise a few young ones."

With that we didn't waste any more time and headed for the town of New Hope.

Because we wanted to travel light we had put Old Pain-in-the-Ass inside the corral with plenty of water and hay to work on. He did watch us ride out and in my mind I had the feeling that he was giving us dirty looks.

47

The town of New Hope was your typical small but well-established western town, that might grow into a larger town or dry up and blow away and only time would tell. It had a general store, livery stable, two saloons, a two-story hotel, a bank, restaurant, schoolhouse, and church. To add to the mix there was lawyer, a doctor and a U.S. Deputy Marshal's office. The stagecoach stopped at Twin Forks every other week, so on the whole, the town was only about a month or two behind the other states in news and several months behind in world news.

So all in all, it was pretty up-to-date when compared to other western towns. Of course there was talk of the railroad coming through New Hope soon. But you couldn't put much stock in that information because in almost every western town there was always talk of the railroad coming through town.

For someone like me it was a nice-looking place. But then, after living in the wilderness and having spent time in Deadwood where most of the town was made up of prospectors with foul mouths and down-and-out drunkards, any civilized town would have looked good.

Our first stop was to see the town's only lawyer so the paperwork could be drawn up, signed, and sent by the next stage to the county courthouse so we could pay our taxes on the transaction and make sure we were listed on the property tax rolls.

The three of us plus Bob and the lawyer walked over to the bank and had our gold weighed so that we could pay off Bob, with the banker and the lawyer as witnesses to the transaction. The remaining gold, along with Mr. Hearst's draft for the sale of our claim, we deposited in the bank with the exception of fifty dollars for each of us for carrying around money, which at that time and age made us look pretty well-off.

Bob separated from us as soon as we left the bank and out in the street we wished him good luck on his new adventure. He headed straight for the general store with his string of mules. He had turned into one more man that was in a big hurry to get to the goldfields, but then it seems that most men are when they have been bitten by the gold fever.

Red was the first to speak and said, "Let's go over to the saloon and toast ourselves on becoming cattle ranchers. I believe we still have some unfinished business to discuss among ourselves."

I had a pretty good idea what was on Red's mind.

At the saloon and over our drinks, Red said, "The way I have it figured a good percentage of those cattle we spotted in that valley are carrying our brand. I say we go after them and at the same time let any other rustlers in the area know that we won't tolerate any rustlers on our range."

Indian and I both agreed that something had to be done and we waited for Red's lead.

"First off," Red said, "we should walk over to the marshal's office and introduce ourselves and tell him about the mixed cattle that were being gathered in that valley we spotted. We'll ask him if he wants to ride along and if he doesn't then we will be on our own but at least he will know our intention."

"Sounds like a good way to go to me," I said. The way I looked at it is if someone takes something that belongs to me without my okay and I don't stand up against it, then I might as well leave the country. I know that times were starting to change and sometime in the near future we would be taking most disputes to the authorities and letting them straighten things out but that time still hadn't made it to the frontier.

When we walked into the marshal's office, we found a man about Red's age sitting behind a desk, with a star pinned on his chest, doing some paperwork.

Looking up, he said, "Hello, gentlemen, what can I do for you?"

Red spoke for the three of us. "Howdy, Marshal, my name is Red and these two men with me are my partners Indian and Dell. We bought Robert Kingsley's ranch and wanted stop by and say hello and tell you something that we spotted on our way to Bob's ranch."

The marshal stood up and I could see that where Red was lean and wiry the marshal was starting to form a roll around his stomach. As he came around the desk he said, "Bob was in a few minutes ago to say goodbye while he was waiting for the general store to fill his order."

As the marshal shook our hands, he said, "The name is James Martin," and then added, "As much as I hate to see Bob leave, I know his heart was no longer into ranching. I think you will find that you have bought yourself a damn good spread, but it will require a little work to get back into shape."

Red said, "We think it will be worth the effort. What we wanted to tell you was that on our way out of Indian Territory, about a day's ride west of Bob's ranch—" Red hesitated for a moment and then corrected himself, "I guess I should now say our ranch, we came across something that was a might peculiar. We spotted five cowboys making a gathering of about eighty or more cattle in a small valley."

The marshal got a frown on his face as he said, "That is strange. You say it was a good day's ride west of your place?"

"Yes, sir."

"There are no ranches that close to Indian Territory other than your spread. A few farmers have tried to farm that land but the Indians have killed some and most of the others have given it up."

Red added, "Bob has told us that he has recently lost some cattle to rustlers. Me and my partners plan on taking a ride over that way and make sure that they don't have any stock with our brand on them. If you would like to accompany us, we would be obliged."

The marshal answered by saying, "I sure as hell would. I was sent down here a couple of months ago to try and stamp out the rustlers and this is the first solid lead I've gotten to date."

"You boys give me half an hour and I'll be ready to go." With that, he walked around the desk and opened a desk drawer and took out three stars and handed one to each of us and said without any fanfare, "You three are now duly sworn-in deputy marshals."

Just as he was about to say more, the door of the office opened and a very good-looking girl, a little bit younger than me, walked in. It was so unexpected that I caught my breath. "Oh, hello Kate," the marshal said, and to us he added, "Gentlemen, this is my daughter Kate." He didn't hesitate as he pointed to each of us and called our names. "This is Red, Indian, and Dell."

When our eyes met they locked for a few seconds. All I could say as I pulled off my hat was, "Miss." I didn't know it at the time but that was the first time that I was to look into the eyes of my future wife and the mother of my children.

The marshal turned to his daughter and said, "Kate, I need you to run on home and tell your mother to pack rations for five men for four days."

I could tell that she was a no-nonsense girl. She didn't waste time asking silly questions of her father as to what was happening. She was out the door in a flash and I felt as if something was missing in the room as soon as she was gone.

The marshal said, "I need to round up one more man and that should only take me a few minutes."

He said he would meet us at the stable and if we didn't mind we should tell the stable man to saddle his and Junior's horses.

As we made our way to the stable Red asked Indian, "What do you think about you taking your horse, and mine as a spare, and ride hard to that valley and check the lay of the land."

All Indian said was it was a hell of a good idea as he mounted up and rode out of town at a fast gallop, leading Red's horse.

Red and I headed for the stable where we told the hostler what the marshal had said about saddling the marshal's and Junior's horses. Red also told him we would need one more horse and saddle because we would be riding with the marshal. The stable man took one look at the stars we were wearing and pointed to a horse that was located in a corner stall and said, "That's the best horse in town. You will also find several saddles back there and you can take your pick."

The stable man wasn't shitting. The horse Red saddled was a fine-looking animal.

The marshal returned with the man he called Junior, who, I was later to learn, owned the general store in town.

When we were mounted, the marshal said, "Red, I seen Indian ride out in a hell of a hurry."

"I asked him to take my horse and scout ahead."

"Is he a good scout?" the marshal asked.

Red answered, with conviction, "The best."

About this time we rode up to the front of the marshal's house and I was hoping I would get to see Kate one more time but when we stopped at the front gate a lady about the same age as the marshal came out carrying three sacks which she passed to him. He in turn handed one to Junior and one to me and kept one himself.

As we were making the sacks secure, I glanced at the window and I saw Kate looking out. My big hope was that she was looking at me but then she was gone before I could be sure.

When we had remounted, the lady took the marshal's hand in hers and said, "You be careful now, James."

The marshal smiled, patted her hand and said "I will Mother." And you could tell, without many words passing between them, that there was a lot of love between them.

We turned our horses and the four of us rode out of New Hope and headed back in the direction of Indian Territory.

48

We kept on the move most of that day, only stopping at water holes to allow the horses to blow and mow a little grass. During the day we made do with jerky and a couple of biscuits that the Marshal's wife had packed for us.

That night we called a halt when it got dark and had our first hot meal since we had left New Hope.

After we had eaten, Junior started to pack up the supplies so that we could move out without delay at first light but, Red said, "Leave the frying pan out along with the bacon and a few of those delicious biscuits if you wouldn't mind, Junior. Dell will fry up some bacon for Indian when he rides in about an hour from now."

Junior looked over at the Marshal who nodded his head yes and then Junior said, "Yes sir."

Knowing Red's uncanny ability to tell certain things, I started to fry the bacon about fifteen minutes before the hour was up with no doubt that Indian would turn up as Red had said. I was just finishing up with the bacon when we heard Indian sing out, "Hello the camp. Don't any of you boys shoot my ass, I'm coming in."

Indian walked into camp leading two very tired horses and turned the horses over to me and said, "If you would water them and stake them out on some fresh grass while I eat, Dell, I would be obliged. I'll hold off telling what I found until you get back. That way I'll only have to tell it once."

I was glad to do it and I was just happy that he was back with us and safe.

When I returned to camp after taking care of the horses, we gathered around Indian to hear what he had found.

Indian said, "When I reached the valley, I found they had pulled out."

"Shit!" the marshal said as he spit into the fire. "Don't tell me that I've missed the sons-of-bitches again."

"I don't think we have lost them just yet, Marshal," Indian said as all eyes turned in his direction.

Red looked at Indian, smiled, and said, "You have more, right?"

"Right, I tracked them for a few miles. They traveled in a southern direction skirting along the edge of Indian Territory. I stayed on their trail until they turned to an east-southeast direction. I figure they will continue in that direction now that they have made a wide berth around any of the ranches they may have rustled cattle from. I hightailed it back here. The way I figure it, if we were to cut across land we could gain a hell of a lot of time on them."

The marshal looked over at Indian with new respect and said, "Son, you did one hell of a good job."

Indian accepted the compliment as if he hadn't heard a word, but I was damn proud of my friend.

The next morning we were up before dawn and eating our morning meal which consisted of biscuits, jerky, and coffee. We saddled up while the night was just starting to turn gray. Before riding out, the marshal turned to Junior and said, "Junior, the two horses that Indian rode while scouting are worn out and we will be pushing our horses hard today. What I would like is for you to give Indian your horse and then take the worn-out horses and follow us at a slower pace. Take your time and stop at each water hole and allow them to rest and eat some before you continue on. They are two fine animals and it would be a shame to lose them over a few no-good rustlers."

If Junior resented the idea of giving up his horse, he didn't show it. I had the feeling that the Marshal and Junior had worked together many times before and that Junior held the Marshal in high esteem. Me, I have to admit I was happy for the two worn-out horses. This morning while we were saddling up, I could see that the two horses Indian had used during his long ride were about shot.

We were soon on our way and around noon we cut the trail but now they were headed due east and we had gained a good day on them. For the rest of the day we followed. We were moving at a good clip but it was hard not to spur our horses on faster. We knew we had to make them last for the long haul ahead.

We continued on until after dark and when we made camp we were all exhausted. We made coffee and had dry jerky for super and then crawled into our bedrolls. We were back up again before the first light and setting round the fire waiting for the coffee. It was a short night. After being very quiet since we had gotten up, the marshal suddenly said, "I believe I know where they are headed."

We all looked over at him and waited for him to explain and he didn't disappoint us. "If I'm guessing right and I think I am, they are going to turn north soon."

"Why north, Marshal?" Red asked.

"They have been making a big circle for the last few days. The only reason for them to do that was so that they could get around the ranches they had been rustling from without being seen. If they turn north soon, they will run into a small railroad spur. All there is there are a few loading pens and a water tower. If they are smart and planning ahead they would have ordered cattle cars to be dropped off on the side track or have them coming when they get there. We could cut across country and if they are heading for the spur, we could make up a lot of time."

"And if they're not headed for the railroad spur, will we lose them?" I asked.

"Not likely. If they are not headed for the railroad spur, then they will have to travel a good sixty miles to find a market for the cattle and we would catch up long before they got that far."

Red said, "I think the railroad spur sounds like a good bet, Marshal. With a phony bill of sale for the cattle, they would be able to ship the cattle back east to a meat packing plant where the meat would be cut up and dispersed in all directions. It would be damn near impossible to trace the cattle or the rustlers from that point on."

With the decision made, it wasn't long after that that we were back on a new trail. With a destination in mind, the ride seemed less tiring.

49

It was a little after noon when the Marshal called a halt and said, "The railroad spur is about a quarter of a mile over that next rise. I think we should move up a little closer and then leave the horses out of sight and make our way on foot to the crest of the hill and look the place over before we ride in."

We continued on slowly until we came to some thick brush where we tied the horses. We left our hats with our gear and started out on foot for the hill crest. About halfway up the small hill we could hear cattle and our excitement mounted. When we neared the top, we got on our hands and knees to make the last few feet.

Below us we had a clear view of the railroad siding. It was made up of three loading pens and a water tank. Alongside the tracks was a pile of railroad ties. The five cowboys had one pen full and were herding the last of the cattle into another pen.

"How are we going to go about this, Marshal?" I asked.

"There is only one thing I can see us doing in open country like this and that is to ride on down there and hope for the best."

"Can I make a suggestion?" Red asked.

"Hell, I'd be happy to listen to anyone."

"I suggest that we let them finish penning those cattle up so that when and if the shooting starts, they won't get in the way. I also think we should put our stars in our pockets. I see no reason to let them know ahead of time that we represent the law until we get down there."

"Sounds okay to me," the Marshal said and added, "We will ride down like we are local cowboys and then identify ourselves. Remember, we have to give them the chance to surrender."

I thought to myself, *There are five of them down there and only four of us, so I didn't see the likelihood of that happening. Now if it had been up to me, I would have opened fire from where we were. If nothing else we could have evened the odds a bit. But things seemed to change when you put on a star.*

We watched the rustlers until they had the last of the cattle in the pens and then we backed off the hill and made our way back to the horses and pocketed our stars.

Once we were mounted and had stars pocketed, the marshal said, "Hell, let's get it done."

We spread out into a line and rode to the top of the hill and over. When we reached the top we slowed to a walk and came off the hill as if we didn't have a care in the world. The rustlers were scattered around the loading pens. One was sitting on the top pole of one of the cattle pens. Three others were standing in the shade of the railroad ties with their backs to the ties smoking. I did a quick sweep with my eyes but couldn't locate the fifth man. I did a bit of swearing under my breath. The missing rustler could be a big problem. As we rode in, I started to mentally look for places where he could be hidden from view. I only came up with one likely spot and that was behind the railroad ties.

By the time I came up with that determination, we were up close to the rustlers. The marshal was the closest to the pile of ties but had turned so that he could keep an eye on the men smoking and at the same time keep an eye on the man sitting on the pen fence.

I was next to the marshal on his left and Red and Indian were on my left. I was just started to ease myself further to my right so that I could get a better angle to keep an eye on the back side of the railroad ties. When I was almost in position, the marshal said, as he pulled his pistol, "I'm Deputy U.S. Marshal James Martin and I'm placing you boys under arrest for suspicion—" That was as far as he got as the fifth rustler stepped out from behind the pile of railroad ties with a cocked pistol pointed at the marshal. I hollered, "Marshal!" and pulled my weapon at the same time but I was a fraction of a second too late and I fired at about the same time as the rustler did. The rustler fell over backwards as the front of his shirt turned red. I knew he was out of the fight, so I didn't waste any more time on him. After that, all hell broke loose. I wanted to glance at the marshal to see if he had been hit but things were moving too fast. I wasn't in a good position to cover the three men next to the railroad ties so I turned my pistol in the direction of the stock pens to try and take out the man that was sitting on the top pole of the corral. When I got him about lined up, I could see I was going to be too late. He had me in his sights and was about to pull the trigger. I was just ready to squeeze the trigger of my weapon, when he fired off a round and I felt a burning sensation on my hip. Before I could return fire, his head exploded and he did a backward somersault off the top railing. Either Red or Indian had beaten me to the shot. I jumped from my horse and ducked behind a big corner post of the corral. As I looked around to find another target, I spotted the three rustlers beating a hasty retreat around the railroad ties. Two seemed to be in good shape but one was hopping on one leg. I snapped off a quick shot but knew I had missed as the limping man threw himself behind the pile of ties.

The whole incident had only lasted a few seconds but I was dripping sweat from my face. Wiping the sweat away on the sleeve of my shirt, I looked around and was relieved to see Red and Indian were behind good cover and both looked okay. The marshal had crawled behind a wooden horse trough that was full of water but I could see that he had blood on his shirt.

Every time one of the rustlers showed himself long enough to throw lead in our direction he would be answered with four rounds from us. After a few minutes the marshal said, "You boys better haul your asses out of there and throw down your weapons. There is no place for you to run and soon we will start working our way around you. You don't stand a chance, so throw out your weapons now and live to see tomorrow."

For a few minutes there was no response from the rustlers and I took the opportunity to reload my pistol. I wasn't all that crazy about leaving my secure location to try and work my way get around to the back side of those the railroad ties. I guess the rustlers weren't too happy with their position either because one of them said "Don't shoot, Marshal, we are coming out." It was a good thing they were giving up because the watering trough the marshal was behind was fast losing its water due to several bullet holes in its side. Without the water in the tank it wouldn't have been much protection.

The marshal called out, "Throw your weapons out first and that includes any knives that you might have. Then back out with your hands high in the air."

Soon after that, three pistols and a couple of knives came flying over the pile of timbers.

"Okay boys, back out from behind those ties with

your hands held high. Any sudden moves and my deputys will shoot," the marshal directed.

Slowly the rustlers came out from behind the pile of railroad ties. "Okay, now I want you to lay down on your stomachs and put your hands behind your back." After they complied with the marshal's directions he turned to me and said, "Dell, would you go over to my saddlebag and bring back three of those handcuffs that I have in there and put them on our friends here."

I did as he asked and when they were snapped into place I could feel the tension start to leave my body.

As soon as we had the three secured, Red asked, "How bad are you hit, Marshal?"

"Not too bad. They got me in the shoulder. I don't think anything is broken. Probably looks more serious than it is but it did seem to have bled pretty damn good."

While Red helped the marshal remove his shirt, Indian tore up two of the sacks that we had carried our supplies in for bandages. As Red was working on the marshal, I walked over to the two rustlers that were down but it was a waste of time, as they were both dead. I removed their weapons and threw them on the pile of weapons that lay in the dirt in front of the railroad ties.

When Red was done with the marshal he looked over at me and glanced down at my hip where some blood had soaked through my pants and said, "You didn't get shot in the ass again did you, Dell?"

I looked over at Indian who had wandered over with a big grin on his face.

I said, "No!" And then added, "I just got nicked on the hip."

"Well drop your pants and let's have a look," Red said.

"I think it's going to be okay, Red."

"Drop your pants, boy. Can't have you getting laid up when we have a herd of cattle that need to be moved back to the ranch. Indian and I don't want to do your share of the work besides our own."

Knowing that if I refused to drop my pants, Red and Indian would only wrestle me down and take them off me and that I would even be more embarrassed, I dropped them.

Indian laughed and said, "You know Red, if Dell would have been turned a little more he would have had a scar on that cheek of his ass to match the scar on the other side."

Red had to laugh and then add injury to my pride by saying, "Damned if you're not right Indian."

While Red was cleaning the wound he said, "Indian, why don't you go over to my saddlebags and get that pint of whiskey that is in there."

When Red said, "Bring the whiskey," while he was working on my wound, I said, "Goddamn it Red, you're not going to pour whiskey on my wound again, are you?"

"Hell no. I'm not about to waste good whiskey on a scratch like that. I figure we could all use a drink about now."

I knew the marshal sure could. He was looking pale and weak. After Red had cleaned and patched my hip he took the bottle over to the marshal who took a long pull and then handed the bottle back to Red and said, "Thanks Red, I really needed that."

After Red had bandaged the wounded rustler's leg, I said, "Red, why don't we move the marshal and the prisoners over under the water tower where there is some shade and I'll get a fire going and make a pot of coffee."

While I was working on the coffee, Indian unsaddled all the horses and put them all in the empty cattle pen.

As we were pouring coffee all around, the marshal asked the youngest prisoner, "What time is the train due to arrive?"

Without thinking the young man said, "Around five this afternoon."

The two other prisoners gave the young man a dirty look but I don't think he even noticed. He was the one with the wounded leg and was probably hoping we would put him on the train so that he could get to where a doctor could take a look at his leg.

After a time of silence and while we enjoyed our coffee, the marshal said, "Boys, I'm sorry, but I think I'm going to have to take the train when it comes in. I won't be worth a damn to help move the cattle with a shot-up shoulder. I'll take the prisoners with me to the next town down the tracks and get them locked up there."

I looked over at the marshal and could tell that he was in no shape to guard three prisoners. One of us was going to have to go with him so that he could get some rest. It was going to be damn hard for three of us to move the cattle back to our ranch. It would be near impossible for two men to get the job done.

I was sitting there wondering how we were going to manage the chore when who should come riding over the hill but Junior, leading Red's horse and riding Indian's. He was a good sight to see. You could tell he was tired but Red's and Indian's horses looked fresh. They had been traveling light and had regained their strength.

When he rode in, I told him to help himself to the coffee and I would take care of the horses.

"Thanks Dell," he said and then headed right over to the marshal to see how he was. As soon as he was satisfied that the marshal was going to be okay, he poured himself a cup of coffee and sat down next to the marshal.

Later, after the marshal dozed off, I filled him in on what had transpired.

While we were waiting for the train to arrive, we made a few plans. Red, Indian, and I would take the marshal's and Junior's horses with us plus the horse Red had rented in Twin Forks. That would give us each an extra mount for the cattle drive back to the ranch. The prisoner's horses and gear would be loaded on the train.

The marshal wanted to leave Junior with us to help with the drive but we vetoed that idea and the marshal finally agreed when Junior sided with us. He was in no shape to travel alone with three prisoners.

We tried to give our deputy marshal's stars back to the marshal but he said we had better keep them until we got the cattle back home. He also added, "With that herd of mixed brands, I would hate to have you boys get shot up as cattle rustlers by one of the ranchers in the area." His foresight turned out to be right on the money.

At about half past five the train pulled in, with five cattle cars and a few passenger cars. After a talk with the marshal, the train conductor decided to take the stock cars back with them rather than leave them on the siding.

After we got the marshal, Junior, and the three prisoners aboard, we loaded the horses of the five rustlers in one cattle car. In another cattle car we placed the two dead rustlers, rolled in their bedrolls.

The three of us waved to the marshal and Junior as the train pulled out then stood there watching until the train was out of sight. There's something about a steam engine that seems to mesmerize children and grown men alike.

50

It was too late in the day to start the drive that evening so we decided to hold off and start the drive early the next day. The horses could certainly handle the extra rest.

At the railroad siding there was a large supply of hay off to one side of the stock pens. We figured it belonged to the railroad and was to be used to feed stock while in the railroad's holding pens. Hell, we had cattle in their holding pens so we made sure the cattle and horses had plenty of hay to work on to keep them happy that evening and through the night. Also, inside each of the corrals was a large tin tank full of water left over from the last rainfall.

With the stock fed and plenty of water available, we had an early meal and then climbed into our sleeping bags while it was still light out. The last few days were short on sleep so we made up for a lot of lost sleep that night.

Early the next morning, we opened the pen gates and let the cattle and spare horses out slowly and started them moving west. We had decided the night before that we wouldn't push the herd hard. They had been pushed pretty hard by the cattle rustlers so when we came to water and good grazing we would let the cattle move at their own pace but always in a westward direction. Hell, a lot of them were our cattle and with winter coming on we didn't want to have them stressed out anymore than they already were.

After about the second day out, one of the steers that carried our brand decided that he should take the lead. I think he had his home range in mind because he set a straight course toward our range. From that time on, we made sure none of the other steers challenged his lead.

It was on our third day of the drive when things changed and it turned out to be for the better. We were slowly moving the herd along when Indian, who had been on point, rode in and pulled up alongside Red. They talked for a few seconds and then Red waved me over.

When I pulled up alongside of Red, he said, "Indian spotted four riders coming in from the northeast. I think we should move over to that side of the herd and meet them as they ride up. Make sure we have our deputy marshal's stars pinned on our chests and in plain sight."

The three of us moved over to that side of the herd and sat on our mounts with about five feet of spacing between us. Red was in the middle with Indian and me flanking him.

The four riders came on and then slowed their pace as they drew near and at the same time fanned out.

They pulled up to a halt about twenty feet in front of us. One of the men was about forty-five and the others ranged from early twenties on down to around sixteen. You could tell at a glance they were family. The younger men were younger versions of the older man. All carried sidearms on their hips, and if they were raised in this part of the country, I'm sure they would know how to use them.

The older man eyeballed us for a moment and nodded at the stars on our chest and said, "You boys the law?"

"Yep," Red answered. "Deputy marshals working under U.S. Marshal James Martin out of New Hope."

"Martin you say? We know him well. I didn't know he had any deputies," the older man said.

"He didn't until a few days ago. We were riding with

him when he caught up with five cattle rustlers at a railroad siding."

"I can see that you got the cattle back but where is the marshal now?" I could see that the old man wasn't all that sure of us yet.

Red continued to do the talking for us. "The marshal was wounded so he and another deputy took the train into the next town."

"What about the rustlers, did they get away?"

"They weren't so lucky. Two rustlers were killed and one took a wound in the leg. The wounded man and the other two decided they had had enough and called it quits."

For the first time, since the man had ridden up, the tension started to relax and the older man smiled and said, "Goddamn that is good news. They have been cutting my herd a few at a time but over the years it all adds up."

After a few more minutes, Red said, "I see you are riding horses that carry the J/4 brand."

"Yes, my three sons and I own the J/4 ranch. My name is Russell Jasper and these are my three sons. We're located north of here."

After the introductions were made all around, Red said, "We have a few head of J/4 stock in the herd. If you're willing to sign for them you can cut them out now. With only three of us, I would be glad to see some of them gone. If not, you can claim them at the former Robert Kingsley ranch. The marshal said he would spread the word around as soon as he returns to New Hope."

"I heard that Bob had sold out to three cowboys, I take it you are them."

After acknowledging that for a fact, the three Jasper

boys and I rode down into the herd and started cutting out the J/4 stock.

By the time we had that done and the Jasper family had their cattle moving in the direction of their range, the day was about over so we moved the cattle until they were on good fresh grass with water near by. We circled the herd after they had their fill of water and they settled down and started mowing grass. The work day seemed to get longer and longer as one of us had to be circling and singing to keep the cattle settled down and not spooked. Needless to say we were very sleep-deprived. I would sometimes find myself dozing off in the saddle during the day and letting my horse do a lot of the work on his own.

On the second day after the Jasper family had taken the cattle, two of the Jasper boys returned with an extra horse each and said their Pa had sent them to help us drive the cattle back to our ranch.

Let me tell you, they were a welcome sight. With two more hands to help with the workload, things got a hell of a lot better in a big hurry.

Indian rode out for a couple of hours that evening and returned with fresh meat and that night we had our first real meal since we had left the railroad siding.

51

Three days later we crested a hill and could see our ranch off in the distance. The five of us gathered there on top of the hill and watched the cattle top the crest and spill over into the valley and spread out below us as if they knew the drive was over and they were home.

We offered to pay the two Jasper boys and cook them a big meal at the ranch house but they turned us down. As the older one put it, "Pa would skin us alive if we were to take money for helping out a neighbor. We will have to pass on the meal also. Pa will be expecting us back to help out in the fall branding."

We shook hands all around and told the boys that when we crossed paths in New Hope we would pay for a big meal and set up the drinks. That, they said, they would accept and then bid us a good-bye and rode off.

We sat there a while longer watching them go, then turned our attention to our ranch.

As we sat there Red said, "Do you boys remember what I said about the cattle drive early this spring when we finished the drive, that all cattle did was shit, piss, and then, on top of all that, you have to put up with them passing gas and stinking up the air."

"It seems I recall you saying something like that," I answered.

Indian added, "I recall you saying exactly those very words, Red."

"Well," Red said as he ignored us and went on to explain himself. "On this drive, I didn't notice any of that kind of unpleasant occurrences."

"Maybe it had something to do with the fact that we own the cattle we were driving," Indian said.

I said, "You know Indian, I think you hit on it. In fact, I noticed a lot of love in Red's singing voice when he rode night herd around the cattle the last few days."

Indian changed the subject by pointing to the ranch and said, "Take a look at who is coming to greet us."

Looking in the direction that Indian had pointed, I could see Old Pain-in-the-Ass headed our way. As soon as he reached us he got in line with us as if we were back on the trail.

"I suppose this means that we are going to have to fix that corral where he probably knocked it down," I said.

Red said, "Seeing how it's your goddamn mule, Dell, I think the repair job will have to be done by you. Indian and I wanted to shoot the goddamn beast but you wouldn't hear about it."

We all had a chuckle over that remark. Down deep, Old Pain-in-the-Ass was like a family member and more so for me as he had saved my life.

As the four of us sat there looking down at our ranch and land, Red said, "Tomorrow one of us going to have to make a ride into New Hope to return the marshal's and Junior's horses along with the one we rented at the livery stable. I would go but at my age, I need to get some rest."

I failed to see the wink that passed between Red and Indian.

Indian said, "I can't go. My back is starting to stiffen up and I plan to sit all day tomorrow in that rocking chair on the front porch and do nothing but rocking, smoking, cussing, and drinking coffee.

I said, "I don't mind taking the ride. I could use a hot

bath in the town bathhouse." As I said that I was thinking, *If I played my cards right, I might get to see the marshal's daughter Kate.*

"I guess the count is in then. Dell, you will have to ride to New Hope tomorrow," Red said, as if he hadn't heard a word I had said.

Indian added, "We know it is a hardship on you Dell, but you will have to do it so there is no use in putting up an argument."

"Damn it, I said I would do it."

I glanced over at Red and Indian and could see them looking at me with big-ass smiles on their faces and I wondered if they knew that the marshal's daughter Kate was on my mind. I don't know how but I'm sure they had it figured out.

I just smiled at them and said, "Go to hell," and at the same time spurred my horse into full speed and headed for the ranch house with a loud rebel yell. Cattle scattered as I came off the hill with Red and Indian right behind me with their own rebel calls while Old Pain-in-the-Ass stayed right there with us as we headed for the ranch yard.